# PERSPECTIVE

## Part One: Love

*Perspective of
love*

## BIJITH K

# Contents

Chapter 1

# Missing

A black moon loomed as Nadia paced, her heart pounding. She'd tried to reach Nilu all day, but her friend's phone was switched off. A few hours before, Nadia had heard strange voices coming from Nilu's house, and now a sense of dread filled her.

"Tariq, I need your help," Nadia pleaded, turning to her husband with desperate eyes. "Something's wrong with Nilu. We have to go check on her."

Tariq scratched his head, a look of skepticism on his face. "You realize Ajith isn't someone to mess with. We shouldn't get involved in their business."

But Nadia was not to be deterred. She fixed Tariq with a steely gaze, her voice low and serious. "If you won't come with me, I'll go alone. And if something happens to me, it'll be on your head."

Tariq sighed, knowing there was no arguing with his stubborn wife. "Alright, but when this turns ugly, remember I tried to talk you out of it."

Nadia nodded, then turned to their son. "If you hear any trouble from Ajith's house, call the police immediately. Understand?"

The boy nodded solemnly, his eyes wide with fear.

Light shone through Ajith's windows. Nadia's heart raced as she rang the doorbell, but only silence greeted them. She tried again, her finger shaking as she pressed the button.

"This is a bad idea," Tariq muttered under his breath. "We should go back."

But Nadia ignored him, reaching for the doorknob. To her surprise, it turned quickly, and the door creaked open.

Inside, darkness greeted them. Nadia flicked the switch and gasped in horror at what she saw.

Ajith lay sprawled on the living room floor, surrounded by empty bottles of Old Monk rum. His beard was matted and tangled, his clothes stained with booze, and God knows what else. At the sound of their entrance, he stirred, his reddened eyes locking onto them with a fierce urgency.

Suddenly, Ajith stirred, his eyes bloodshot and wild. He stumbled to his feet and scratched his unkempt beard. Without a word, he staggered past Nadia and her husband, disappearing into the garage. Moments later, the sound of a car engine roared to life, and Ajith sped away into the night.

Nadia called out for Nilu, her voice trembling with fear. As she searched the house, a strange humming noise caught her attention. She followed the sound to the laundry room, where the washing machine was running.

She pushed open the door and froze, chills racing through her body like frozen needles. The washing machine was running, but it was filled with something else entirely instead of clean clothes.

With shaking hands, Nadia lifted the lid, a scream tearing from her throat at the sight that greeted her. Inside, Anvi's clothes floated in a sea of crimson; the water stained a sickening shade of red.

Nadia's vision swam, the room spinning around her as she collapsed to the floor in a dead faint. Tariq rushed to her side, his face pale with shock and horror.

With trembling fingers, he dialed the police, his voice shaking as he begged them to hurry. Then he called for an ambulance, praying his wife would be okay.

*****

Nadia's eyes fluttered open, the harsh lights of the hospital room blinding her momentarily. The heart monitor beeped as she oriented herself. Tariq sat beside her, worry etched on his face.

"What happened?" Nadia croaked, her throat dry and scratchy.

"You collapsed," her husband explained, gently squeezing her hand. "The police are investigating Nilu's disappearance and the blood-stained clothes in the washing machine. A news channel also came to the hospital this morning and interviewed me about Nilu's disappearance."

Nadia's eyes widened, her heart racing. "What did you tell them?"

"I told them the truth," Tariq said, his voice steady. "I explained how we found Ajith drunk, and how we discovered the blood-stained clothes in the washing machine. Given Ajith's erratic behavior, I also mentioned that we had been worried about Nilu's safety for some time."

Nadia nodded, her mind reeling with the implications of Tariq's words.

Nadia's heart sank as the memories came flooding back. She reached for the remote control, her fingers trembling as she switched on the television on the wall opposite her bed.

The news anchor's face filled the screen, his expression grim. "Breaking news: Famous actress Nilu has been reported missing. Police are currently investigating her disappearance and have named her husband, Ajith, as a person of interest."

The camera cut to a crowd of Nilu's fans gathered outside her house, displaying signs with pictures. Many were in tears, their faces contorted with grief and worry.

"Nilu's fans have been holding vigils outside her home, praying for her and her daughter's safe return," the anchor continued. "The actress, known for her captivating performances and kind heart, has touched the lives of many."

Nadia watched, her heart laden with guilt and fear. She should have protected her friend and seen the signs earlier.

As the news report continued, Nadia's mind drifted to Anvi, Nilu's daughter. Where was she in all of this? Was she safe?

The camera showed Nilu's co-stars speaking gravely to reporters. "We're all praying for Nilu's safe return," one actress said, her voice trembling. "She's not just a colleague, but a dear friend to all of us."

The news report continued. "Breaking news: Nilu's best friend Nadia has made a troubling discovery. We go live to Inspector Daniel's media address."

The camera cut to Inspector Daniel, standing grim-faced before the press as flashbulbs popped. "A few hours ago, Mr. Tariq, who is Nadia's husband, came to us with a piece of evidence she found while searching for her missing friend. It appears to be an article of clothing belonging to Nilu's child."

He held up a plastic evidence bag containing a small, bloodstained shirt. Gasps rippled through the crowd. "We have sent a sample of this cloth to the lab for analysis, but the presence of blood raises serious concerns about the well-being of both Nilu and her child. My team won't stop until we solve this and bring them home safely.

Inspector Daniel left the podium as reporters burst into frenzied discussion.

*****

The same day, Nadia was discharged from the hospital. As Tariq drove her home, she stared out the window, her mind consumed with thoughts of Nilu and Anvi.

When they arrived home, Nadia couldn't bear to be inside. She stepped out into the backyard and sank into a chair; her eyes fixed on Nilu's house across the street. Police cars lined the driveway, their lights flashing silently. Officers in uniform moved in and out of the house.

Nadia watched them work, her heart heavy with worry and guilt. If only she'd seen the warning signs sooner. Being a better friend might have kept Nilu and Anvi safe.

Lost in thought, Nadia didn't notice the muscular officer until he stood before her. She looked up, startled to find a familiar face.

"Mrs. Nadia?" the man asked, his voice deep and authoritative.

Nadia nodded, her throat suddenly dry.

"I'm Inspector Daniel," he said, extending his hand. "I'm leading the investigation into Nilu's disappearance."

Nadia shook his hand, her own trembling slightly. "It's nice to meet you, Inspector," she said, her voice barely above a whisper.

Inspector Daniel took a seat beside her, his eyes scanning the backyard before settling on Nadia. "How are you feeling, Mrs. Nadia?" he asked, his tone surprisingly gentle.

Nadia took a deep breath, trying to steady herself. "I'm okay," she said, her voice stronger now. "Just worried about Nilu and Anvi. I can't imagine what they must be going through."

Inspector Daniel nodded, his expression serious. "We're doing everything we can to find them," he assured her. "But we could use your help. You know Nilu better than anyone."

Nadia hesitated for a moment, then nodded. "Of course," she said. "Anything I can do to help."

She stood up, gesturing towards the house. "Would you like to come inside for some tea, Inspector? We can talk more comfortably there."

Inspector Daniel nodded, rising to his feet. "That would be great, thank you."

Nadia took a deep breath as she sat across from Inspector Daniel in the living room.

"Mis, Nadia," Inspector Daniel began, his voice calm but firm. "I understand you've been through a lot, but I need you to tell me everything you know about Nilu's disappearance."

Nadia nodded, her eyes welling up with tears. "Nilu and I... we were more than just friends. She confided in me; told me things she couldn't tell anyone else."

She paused, collecting herself before continuing. "Nilu was lonely, Inspector. Despite her fame and success, she felt trapped in her own life. She would come to me to escape, to feel like herself again."

Inspector Daniel leaned forward, his brow furrowed. "What do you mean by trapped?"

"Her marriage to Ajith," Nadia explained, her voice tinged with bitterness. "Nilu said she felt like she was just playing a role, pretending to be the perfect mother to Anvi. But Ajith... he didn't care about her. He was always too busy with work, and when he wasn't working, he was drinking."

She shook her head, anger flashing in her eyes. "Nilu had dreams, Inspector. She wanted a husband who would love her, cherish her, and take her on adventures. But instead, she got Ajith. An alcoholic, irresponsible man who couldn't even be bothered to spend time with his own family."

Nadia's voice broke as she continued. "Nilu felt utterly alone, Inspector. The only time she felt any joy was when Anvi came home from her lessons. But even then, it was fleeting. She deserved so much better than the life she had. The day before yesterday, I got a call from Nilu; She was crying, telling me about how Ajith had struck and assaulted her the previous day. I tried to reassure her, told her that everything would be okay, that we could admit Ajith to a deaddiction center."

She paused, taking a deep breath as tears welled up in her eyes. "But now, with the bloody cloth of Anvi... I can't forget it, Inspector. I never thought this would happen to them."

Nadia broke down, sobs wracking her body as she buried her face in her hands. The image of the bloodstained shirt flashed through her mind, a haunting reminder of the horror that had befallen her best friend and her child.

"I thought... even though Ajith was a drinker, I never imagined he would do something like this," Nadia managed to say between sobs. "He's more cruel than I ever realized."

Inspector Daniel handed her a tissue, his face filled with concern. Nadia wiped her eyes, her breathing shallow and shaky.

"I need some water," Nadia said quietly, her voice barely above a whisper. She felt drained physically and emotionally as the weight of the situation pressed down on her.

Inspector Daniel nodded, rising from his seat to fetch her a glass. Nadia leaned back against the couch, closing her eyes as she tried to compose herself.

Questions swirled in her mind, each one more terrifying than the last.

She knew she had to stay strong, for Nilu's sake. She had to do everything possible to help Inspector Daniel find them and bring them home safely. But the fear and uncertainty were almost more than she could bear.

As Inspector Daniel returned with the water, Nadia took a sip, the cool liquid soothing her parched throat. She looked up at the Inspector, her eyes pleading.

"Please, Inspector," she whispered, her voice barely audible. "Please find them. Bring them home safe. I... I don't know what I'd do if something happens to them."

Inspector Daniel nodded, his expression softening. "I understand, Ms. Nadia. I appreciate your cooperation. We'll do everything in our power."

Nadia took a deep breath, trying to calm her racing heart as Inspector Daniel left her house. She sank back into the couch, her body shaking with sobs as the weight of the situation crashed down upon her once more.

Nadia closed her eyes, trying to block out the horrifying thoughts that threatened to overwhelm her.

After what felt like an eternity, Nadia's sobs subsided, leaving her feeling drained and empty. She wiped her eyes with the back of her hand, shuddering as she tried to compose herself.

She grabbed the remote and turned on the TV, searching for news. Her heart sank as Nilu's image filled the screen.

The news anchor's face filled the screen, her expression somber as she delivered the latest update on Nilu's disappearance.

"In a shocking turn of events, our news team has uncovered disturbing information about Dr. Ajith. We have an exclusive interview with one of the nurses who works closely with Dr. Ajith."

The camera cuts to an interview, showing a nurse. "Dr. Ajith is not the man everyone thinks he is," she says, her voice trembling slightly. "He's short-tempered and inflexible with his shifts. He always leaves the hospital at 4 o'clock sharp, no matter what."

The nurse pauses briefly before continuing. "He's just working for the money. He's not interested in his professional job. I've heard him tell other nurses that he wants to drink alcohol and needs to go to the bar after 4 o'clock."

"This revelation raises serious concerns about Dr. Ajith's professionalism. Our team will continue to investigate this matter and bring you updates as they become available."

"Stay tuned for more on this developing story. We'll be right back after a short break."

## At the Bar

Ajith hunched over the bar counter, which reeked of stale smoke and cheap booze. His eyes were fixed on the TV, where a news anchor discussed Nilu's disappearance. He gulped more whiskey, feeling it burn down his throat.

Suddenly, the door to the bar burst open, and a group of men stormed in, their faces contorted with anger.

"There he is!" one of the men shouted, pointing an accusing finger at Ajith. "The bastard!"

Ajith lurched up, alcohol clouding his sight. He clutched his bottle like a weapon as the men charged, fists raised in rage.

In a flash, Ajith swung the bottle, smashing the glass against the lead assailant's skull. The man crumpled to the ground, glass shards and blood splattering across the floor. Ajith seized a chair, using it defensively against the charging men.

The bar erupted into chaos as Ajith fought back, his drunken strikes landed true. He smashed the chair against one man's chest, sending him flying into a table. Another rushed him, but Ajith dodged, snatched a pool cue and smashed it across his back.

Despite his inebriated state, Ajith 's instincts kicked in, his years of training as a doctor gave him an edge in the brawl. He knew where to strike, how to use his opponents' momentum against them, and when to retreat and regroup.

Ajith stood over the fallen attacker amid the bar's wreckage, panting with bloody knuckles. He stumbled back to the counter for more whiskey, tossing cash to the stunned bartender hiding behind it.

"For the damages," he said, his voice rough. "And another whiskey, if you don't mind.", his eyes once again fixed on the television screen, where his own face stared back at him, a wanted man in a city consumed by the mystery of his wife's disappearance.

Ajith staggered through the bar's debris. His fallen opponent stirred with a groan, spotting him through dazed eyes and letting out a hoarse yell as he left.

"Don't let him out!" the man shouted, his voice filled with anger and desperation. "He's that monster Ajith - what he did to Nilu and her baby!"

The words froze the room. Ajith stopped at the door, turning to scan the crowd with bloodshot eyes. Everyone shrank back.

"Keep silent," he growled.

He nodded at his beaten opponents, sending fear through the room. The trembling bartender rushed him a fresh whiskey, eager to avoid more trouble.

Ajith grabbed the bottle, spitting the cork with his teeth, and yanked it down. He gulped the whiskey, its sharp scent filling the air.

He left without a word, the bar frozen behind him. Outside, he stumbled to his black car and slumped into the driver's seat after fumbling with the lock.

# Chapter 2

# The Police

Inspector Daniel sat at his desk in the police station, his brow furrowed as he mulled over the events of his search. The discovery of Anvi's phone weighed heavily on his mind, a crucial piece of evidence that could potentially break the case wide open. The device yielded easily to Daniel's team when they tried her birthdate as the passcode, granting them immediate access to its contents.

Sinking into his seat, he massaged his forehead wearily. The media circus surrounding the disappeared teenager had intensified, and he understood that revealing details about the found phone would only add fuel to the growing flames.

A knock interrupted his brooding. "Come in," he called out, straightening his posture.

The door opened and Sub-Inspector Akhil stepped in. "Sir, I have an update on the evidence we collected."

Inspector Daniel motioned for him to take a seat. "What have you got?"

Akhil handed over a file. "We've confirmed that the phone belongs to Anvi".

Daniel nodded, going over the pages. "Good job, Akhil. But listen closely – we have to keep this phone secret for now. The last thing we want is for the news outlets to find out and start spreading their own sensational stories."

Akhil hesitated, then asked, "But sir, don't you think the public has a right to know? It might assist us in gathering additional information."

Inspector Daniel shook his head. "You know how these media vultures operate. They'll twist the facts, add their own flair, and turn it into a circus. All they care about is views and ratings, not the truth."

Akhil nodded, his expression somber. "Yes, sir. I'll make sure the team keeps it under wraps."

Inspector Daniel dismissed Akhil with a nod. "Leave the phone and wait outside. I'll examine it."

Akhil gave him the bagged phone and left for the break room to get tea.

Meanwhile, inside his office, Inspector Daniel carefully took the phone out of the evidence bag and examined it closely. His eyes remained fixed on Anvi's phone as he scrolled through her messages and social media profiles.

Exploring her digital life revealed a very introverted girl. Her interactions were limited, and she spent most of her time immersed in online gaming and communicating with others through a Discord platform. The app's anonymity allowed users to adopt fake identities, making it difficult to identify the people she talked to.

As he navigated through her chat history, two names stood out: Nikhil and Sentinel. Anvi's conversations with Nikhil were particularly intriguing. The two had met while playing games together. They had developed a close bond, sharing everything from their daily lives to pictures of each other.

One exchange caught Inspector Daniel's attention. Anvi had sent a message to Nikhil, saying, "I can't believe you beat me again! You're too good at this game. I demand a rematch!" Nikhil had replied with a series of laughing emojis, followed by, "Anytime, anywhere. I'll always be ready to take you on!"

Their playful banter made Anvi's disappearance seem even grimmer.

He called out to his subordinate to call Sub-Inspector Akhil.

Akhil entered the room, his eyebrows raised in anticipation. "Yes, sir?"

Inspector Daniel handed him the phone. "I need you to find out everything you can about this Nikhil's character," Inspector Daniel instructed, handing over the phone. "These chats could be crucial in locating him. I want a full report on his background and whereabouts."

Akhil nodded, taking the phone. "Right away, sir. I'll get on it immediately."

As Akhil turned to leave, the Inspector held up his hand. "Wait, give me the phone back for a moment. I need to go through this Sentinel's profile as well."

Akhil returned the phone back to the inspector, who quickly took a screenshot of the relevant messages. "Alright, now go and investigate Nikhil. Report back to me as soon as you have any information."

"Yes, sir!" Akhil saluted and left, intent on uncovering Nikhil's identity.

Inspector Daniel delved deeper into the mysterious relationship between Anvi and the enigmatic Sentinel. As he read their messages, patterns surfaced. It became evident that Anvi had known Sentinel long before she started talking to

Nikhil. The Sentinel kept his identity concealed, but he always spoke to her with the warmth and affection of a brother.

Anvi confided in Sentinel more than anyone else, sharing her thoughts, fears, and dreams. Still, she never revealed her relationship with Nikhil to him. It was as if she kept that part of her life separate, treasuring the special bond with her virtual sibling.

Daniel's eyes widened as he read a specific exchange between the two. Anvi had asked Sentinel to share something about himself, but he politely declined, keeping his mystery intact. However, he did mention the possibility of having a girlfriend, stressing that his connection with Anvi was completely platonic—a brother-sister relationship built on trust and understanding.

It became clear to Daniel that Sentinel had consistently supported Anvi, especially when her parents were distant and uncommunicative. Sentinel's humor and charm filled the void in her life, becoming her best friend, brother, and family all in one.

As Daniel kept reading, he came across Avni's heartfelt confession. She admitted that she liked Sentinel more than anyone else in the world.

The chat between Anvi and Sentinel puzzled him further. Daniel summoned another sub-inspector and handed over the phone.

"I need you to gather all information you can on this Sentinel character," Daniel instructed. "I've already assigned Sub-Inspector Akhil to investigate Nikhil, so your focus should be solely on Sentinel."

The sub-inspector took the phone to examine it. Daniel leaned on his desk as he spoke.

"I can't find any concrete information about Sentinel," he admitted, frustration clear in his voice. "But we can't rule out the possibility that he might have ulterior motives."

"I need you to dig deep," Daniel emphasized, his voice low and serious. "Don't hesitate to ask if you need any assistance or resources for this case. This is a top priority."

The sub-inspector pocketed the phone and left to investigate Sentinel.

He quickly grabbed his phone and dialed the number of another sub-inspector.

"Sub-Inspector Vijay," he commanded into the receiver, his voice firm. "What's the status of your investigation into Ajith? Have you found anything yet?"

On the other end of the line, Vijay's voice crackled with static. "Sir, we've been working around the clock, but Ajith seems to have vanished. We've checked his usual haunts, but no one has seen him."

Daniel's jaw clenched, his frustration mounting. "Listen to me carefully, Vijay. I need you to find Ajith as soon as possible. The media and Nilu's fans are breathing down our necks, demanding answers. He may be behind all of this, but we're in deep trouble until we bring him in for questioning."

The inspector's voice grew louder, his tone sharp and commanding. "I want you to double your efforts. When I come to my desk tomorrow morning, I expect to see the news on TV reporting that the police have arrested Ajith. Do you understand?"

Vijay's voice wavered slightly as the weight of Daniel's words sank in. "Yes, sir. I understand. We'll do everything in our power to find him."

"Good," Daniel replied, his voice stern. "Now get back to work. Time is of the essence."

After hanging up, Daniel leaned back, deep in thought. Nilu's case needed to be solved. Determined, he grabbed the phone once more, ready to use every resource to catch Ajith.

Daniel slammed down the phone in frustration.

"Where's that drunk Ajith?" he muttered. "Probably at a bar."

He scanned through possible hideouts in the city. Time was short to find Nilu and her daughter.

At the station, Daniel studied Nilu's case files, glaring at Ajith's bar fight report.

"How did he slip away?" He slammed the file down, making his subordinates jump. "Find him now!"

"Sir," the Sub-Inspectors stammered, "we've searched everywhere but didn't find any trace".

*****

# Nikhil

Daniel's eyes narrowed. "And what about this Nikhil? Have we located him yet?"

Akhil nodded. "Yes, sir. We've found his address. He's a student."

"Good. Let's pay him a visit." Daniel strode out of the station, his team scrambling to keep up.

Nikhil sat on his couch, eyes puffy from crying when Inspector Daniel's team arrived unannounced.

"I just can't believe it," Nikhil snifled, wiping his nose with the back of his hand. "Anvi.......It's all so horrible."

Daniel leaned in. "Nikhil, we need your help. You might know something important."

Nikhil nodded, taking a deep breath. "Anvi and I met online through a gaming community. We hit it off right away and started talking every day. She was terrific, you know? Smart, funny, kind. I... I think I was falling for her."

Daniel's expression softened slightly. "And what about this Sentinel? We understand Anvi introduced you to him as well."

Nikhil's eyes widened. "Sentinel? Yeah, he was part of our group—a real mystery, that one. Never shared any personal details, always kept to himself. But he was cool, you know? Like a little brother to us. Anvi really liked him."

Daniel nodded, jotting down notes. "And you have no idea who he really is? No clues about his identity?"

Nikhil shook his head. "No, sir. He was always careful about that. Said he preferred to stay unknown."

Daniel sighed, leaning back in his chair. "Alright, Nikhil. I appreciate your help. Please let us know if you think of anything else, anything at all."

As the inspector and his team prepared to leave, Nikhil's voice stopped them. "Please, sir. Find whoever did this. Find Ajith and make him pay. Anvi... she deserves justice."

Daniel met Nikhil's tearful gaze, his own eyes hardening with determination. "We will, Nikhil. I promise you that."

# Chapter 3

# The Case That Ate Its Tail

At sunrise, Daniel paced his office, frustrated and exhausted. Three days into Nilu and her daughter's disappearance, the case had stalled while media coverage exploded with speculation.

His phone buzzed nonstop, with reporters and superiors demanding updates he couldn't provide. The pressure bore down on him, threatening to crush him.

Outside the police station, a crowd of Nilu's fans had gathered, their anger and impatience palpable. They chanted and waved signs demanding justice for their star, burning effigies of Ajith and the police in rage.

As the clock struck eight, Daniel's patience finally snapped. He stormed out of his office, his eyes blazing with barely contained fury. The sub-inspectors and constables scattered, their heads bowed low to avoid his gaze.

"Three days!" Daniel roared, slamming his fist against the wall. "Three miserable days, and what have we accomplished? Absolutely nothing!"

The officers shufled their feet, their eyes downcast. They knew the gravity of the situation, the pressure mounting with each passing hour.

"Sir," one of the sub-inspectors ventured, his voice trembling slightly. "We've worked nonstop, but Ajith's vanished like a ghost."

Daniel whirled around, his finger jabbing at the young officer's chest. "Ghost? He's a man, not a supernatural being! And it's your job to find him, no matter how well he's hidden himself."

The sub-inspector swallowed hard, his face paling under Daniel's intense scrutiny. "Yes, sir. We'll ramp up our efforts."

Daniel's gaze swept across the room, his disappointment and frustration evident in every line of his face. "You better, because if we don't find Ajith soon, there's a very real possibility that Nilu and her daughter are already dead."

The words hung heavy in the air, their implication settling like a suffocating blanket over the room.

"And if that happens," Daniel continued, his voice low and dangerous, "it won't just be Ajith facing the consequences. I've been told in no uncertain terms that if we don't make progress, the higher-ups are ready to replace the entire investigation team."

A collective gasp swept through the room, with the officers' eyes widening in shock and fear.

Daniel's shoulders drooped, his energy fading. He rubbed his face, exhaustion clearly showing in his features.

"I know you're all doing your best," he said, his voice softening a bit. "But our best isn't enough right now. We need to be better, faster, smarter. We need to think outside the box."

The officers nodded with renewed determination. They understood the stakes and couldn't surrender, not with lives at risk.

"Alright, back to work," Daniel ordered, his voice regaining its steely edge. "Updates hourly, and report any findings immediately."

The officers dispersed, footsteps fading as they rushed to their duties. Daniel stared at the crowd outside the station, their angry shouts and jeers echoing off the walls. His brow furrowed as he took in the scene - Nilu's fans had amassed in force, waving signs and burning effigies in outrage over the lack of progress.

*****

Usually, such demonstrations wouldn't bother him, but today their anger only increased the stress weighing him down. He couldn't blame them for their frustration and impatience - he constantly felt the same pressure inside. If only they knew how tirelessly his team was working, examining every lead, pursuing any possible clue to Ajith's whereabouts.

Daniel's eyes narrowed at a taxi pulling up in the rain. The crowd jeered louder as Ajith emerged, his face twisted in anguish.

The crowd surged forward, their anger boiling over into violence. Stones and debris rained down on the taxi, shattering windows and denting metal. Ajith cowered in the backseat, his hands raised in a futile attempt to protect himself.

Daniel orders his officers to control the crowd. They formed a human barrier, pushing back against the sea of enraged faces. But the crowd's fury knew no bounds. A stick hurtled through the air, striking Ajith on the head. Blood poured from the wound, mixing with the rain and running down his face in crimson rivulets.

Daniel fought his way through the chaos, pulse hammering against his rib. He reached the taxi just as Ajith stumbled out, his face a mask of pain and desperation. The rain washed the blood from his body, but it did little to cleanse the anguish etched into his features.

With the help of his officers, Daniel managed to push through the crowd and drag Ajith into the station. The man collapsed at Daniel's feet, his body wracked with sobs. He clung to Daniel's legs, his words tumbling out in a desperate plea.

"I can't live like this anymore," Ajith cried, his voice raw with emotion. "I can't bear the weight of this guilt, this pain. I was an alcoholic, yes, but it was for a reason. You have to believe me, Inspector. I didn't do this. I could never hurt Nilu or our daughter."

Daniel stared down at the broken man before him, his mind racing. Every piece of evidence they had gathered pointed to Ajith's guilt. The bloodstained clothes, the suspicious behaviour, the sudden disappearance. It all added up to a damning picture.

Daniel's instincts told him to be cautious, not to let his guard down. He had seen too many criminals try to manipulate their way out of a tight spot. But there was something about Ajith's plea that tugged at his heartstrings.

Without a word, Daniel hauled Ajith to his feet and led him to the interrogation room. He sat the man down in a chair, his eyes never leaving Ajith's face. Cold fluorescent lights cast harsh shadows across the room.

## Painted lies?

Daniel stared at Ajith, his eyes narrowing with suspicion. The man's pleas and sobs failed to sway Daniel's resolve.

"Enough with the drama, Ajith," Daniel said, his voice cold and unforgiving. "We both know you never loved Nilu. You were cruel to her and your daughter, making their lives a living hell. How can you sit there and claim innocence when all the evidence points to your guilt?"

Ajith's sobs intensified, his body shaking with the force of his emotions. "Please, Inspector, you have to believe me. I know I was a terrible husband and father, but I could never hurt them like this. I loved them, in my way."

Daniel scoffed, his lips curling into a sneer. "Love? Is that what you call it? Nilu had a pathetic life because of you, Ajith. She was trapped in a marriage with a man who cared more about his next drink than his own family."

Ajith's eyes widened, a flicker of anger flashing behind the tears. "You don't know anything about our marriage, Inspector. You don't know the struggles we faced."

Daniel leaned forward, his face inches from Ajith's. "I know enough. I know that you're a perfect actor, able to turn on the waterworks and play the victim when it suits you, but I see through your lies, Ajith. I know you're the villain in this story."

Ajith's shoulders drooped, and his head hung down. "I swear, Inspector, I didn't do this. Over the past few days, I've been trying to locate Nilu and Anvi, searching everywhere and following every lead available."

Daniel's eyebrows shot up, a hint of disbelief in his voice. "Is that so? Then how do you explain the bloody clothes we found in your house? The evidence doesn't lie, Ajith."

Ajith's face paled, his eyes widening with fear. " I can't explain it. But I swear on my life, I didn't hurt them."

Daniel narrowed his eyes, studying Ajith's face intently. The man's words rang hollow, his excuses feeble at best. Daniel had witnessed countless criminals attempt to escape through deception and theatrics.

"The bloody clothes were there when you reached home, you say?" Daniel scoffed, his disbelief evident. "And what, you just happened to overlook them? Forgive me if I find that hard to believe."

Ajith's eyes widened, and his mouth moved as if gasping for air. "I... I don't know how they ended up there," he stammered. "But I swear, I didn't cause any harm."

Daniel stood up, his chair scraping against the floor. He towered over Ajith, his presence intimidating and overwhelming. "I don't believe you, Ajith. The evidence is stacked against you, and your words mean nothing. All you need to do is admit the truth. Admit that you're the one who did this to your family."

Ajith's eyes darted around the room, his breath coming in short, panicked gasps. "No, no, no. I can't admit to something I didn't do. Please, Inspector, you have to believe me. I'm not the villain here."

Daniel's patience was thin, his frustration mounting with each passing second. He slammed his hand down on the table, the sound echoing through the room like a gunshot. "Enough! I've had it with your lies and your games. You're not fooling anyone, Ajith. The evidence speaks for itself."

Ajith's body seemed to deflate, his shoulders sagging under the weight of Daniel's accusations. He buried his face in his hands, his sobs echoing through the room. "I didn't do it," he whispered, his voice barely audible above the sound of his tears. "I didn't do it."

Daniel shook his head, his eyes hard and unforgiving. He knew he had Ajith right where he wanted him, backed into a corner with nowhere to run. It was only a matter of time before the man cracked under the pressure, before he admitted to the heinous crimes he had committed.

"Please, Inspector, you have to listen to me," Ajith begged, his hands clasped together in supplication. "I came here to surrender, to cooperate with the investigation. I don't want to waste any more time."

Daniel leaned back in his chair, his arms crossed over his chest. He studied Ajith's face, searching for any hint of deception. "Go on," he said, his voice cold and unforgiving.

Ajith took a deep breath, his eyes fixed on the table before him. "When I got home from work that day, I was shocked to find Anvi's clothes in the washing machine. They were covered in blood, and I knew something terrible had happened."

He leaned forward, his elbows resting on the table.

And what did you do then?

Ajith's shoulders slumped, his head hanging low. "I panicked. I started drinking, trying to numb the pain and the fear. I knew no one would believe me, that they would all think I had something to do with their disappearance."

Daniel's jaw clenched, his patience wearing thin. "So, you thought drinking was the answer? Instead of coming to the police and reporting your wife and daughter missing, you decided to drown your sorrows in alcohol?"

Ajith's eyes filled with tears, his voice trembling as he spoke. "I was a coward, Inspector. I was afraid of facing the truth, of admitting that I had failed as a husband and a father. I thought I could find them on my own, that I could search the world until I brought them home."

Daniel sneered and asked, "So, Ajith, how did that turn out? Did you find them and bring them back safely?"

Ajith shook his head, his tears falling freely now. "No, Inspector. I realized that I was only making things worse, that the police were closing in on me. I didn't want to waste any more time, so I decided to surrender."

Daniel's eyes flashed with anger, his fists clenching at his sides. He stood up abruptly, his chair scraping against the floor. "You expect me to believe that, Ajith? You expect me to believe that you're innocent, that you had nothing to do with their disappearance?"

Ajith's eyes widened, his hands raised in a gesture of surrender. "I swear, Inspector, I didn't do anything to them. I love my wife and daughter, even if I haven't always shown it."

Daniel's hand shot out, grabbing Ajith by the collar and hauling him to his feet. He slammed the man against the wall, his face inches from Ajith's. "Love? You call this love? Abandoning your family, drinking

You're putting yourself into a stupor, and then coming here with some half-baked story about how you're innocent?"

Ajith's face crumpled, his body sagging against the wall. "Please, Inspector, you have to believe me. I know I've made mistakes, but I would never hurt them."

Daniel's fist connected with Ajith's face, the impact echoing through the room. Ajith's head snapped back, blood trickling from his split lip. "Don't lie to me, Ajith. Don't you dare lie to me."

Ajith's eyes fluttered closed, his breath coming in short, pained gasps. "I'm not lying, Inspector. I swear on my life, I'm telling the truth."

Daniel's eyes bore into Ajith's, his gaze unwavering and intense. He leaned forward, his hands clasped tightly in front of him. "Look, Ajith, I can't believe you. When I've found the villain, I won't send my team on a wild goose chase."

Ajith's eyes widened, desperation visible on his face. "Please, Inspector, I can prove my innocence. But I need your help to investigate further. Don't waste any more time assuming I'm guilty."

Daniel hesitated for a moment, his mind racing. He knew that every second counted in a case like this and couldn't afford to overlook any potential leads. With a heavy sigh, he turned to his assistant. "Find any lead you can, no matter how small. We'll continue the investigation, even if it means working day and night."

The assistant nodded and hurried out of the room to relay Daniel's orders to the rest of the team. Daniel turned back to Ajith, his eyes narrowing. "Alright, Ajith. I'm giving you a chance to explain yourself. But if I don't believe your story, you'll be the prime suspect,"

"Inspector, please try to understand. I love Nilu and Anvi more than anything in this world," Ajith said, his hands trembling. "But everything has changed. All because of my failure as a husband."

Daniel leaned forward, his voice stern. "I know you were a terrible husband, Ajith. How can you possibly prove that you loved Nilu?"

Ajith's eyes welled with tears, his voice barely a whisper. "Do you know something, Inspector? Nilu was not just my wife. She was the only girl I ever loved."

He closed his eyes, lost in a memory. "I can still feel her footsteps when she approached me. Her steps were etched in my heart. The way she dragged her shoes while wandering across the campus, her footsteps made my heart beat faster."

Ajith's voice grew wistful, a hint of a smile on his lips. "I can sense her smell even now. It would make my heart melt. And her eyes... they could make my heart stops beating. Her single moment of sadness could break my heart into pieces. I couldn't handle her presence, sir."

He looked down, his voice tinged with regret. "But I never knew how to love someone. The act of making love like other guys."

Daniel's patience wore thin, his voice sharp. "Enough with the drama, Ajith."

Ajith broke down, his sobs echoing through the room. "You don't believe me, do you? No one does."

"Alright, Ajith," Daniel said, his voice cold and stern. "You say you want to tell me everything. So start from the beginning."

Ajith took a deep breath, his hands clenched tightly in front of him. "It all started when I first met Nilu on campus. She was the most beautiful girl I had ever seen."

Daniel's eyebrows shot up, a flicker of surprise crossing his face. He had always assumed that Ajith and Nilu's marriage was one of convenience, not love. But he kept his thoughts to himself, motioning for Ajith to continue.

Ajith's voice cracked, his shoulders shaking with sobs. Daniel watched him closely, his mind racing. He knew that Ajith's story could be a carefully crafted lie designed to throw him off the scent. But something about the man's raw emotion felt genuine, almost too painful to be an act.

Daniel reached into his pocket, pulling out a recording device. He placed it on the table between them, his finger hovering over the button. "Ajith, I'm going to record your story. Every word you say will be used as evidence, so choose your words carefully."

Daniel leaned forward, his eyes narrowing as he pressed the button on the recording device. The soft whir of the tape filled the room, a reminder that every word spoken could make or break the case.

Chapter 4

# Cupid's Arrow

I never experienced love after my parents died during my childhood. I was left with my uncle, who only took me in so he could inherit my father's property. But I was merely there for the sake of being in that house.

My uncle's house had been a cold, unwelcoming place where I was little more than a burden to be tolerated. His daughter, my cousin, was their cherished, sheltered child. And I? I was the lowly weed, to be kept at a distance lest I sully her perfection.

As the years passed, I retreated further into the safety of my books, losing myself in the adventures and romances that filled their pages. There, I found the companionship I craved, the love that had been so cruelly denied me. Yet, while I lost myself in fiction, I yearned to live those adventures myself.

Nilu and I met in Chennai during college. After finishing school in Kerala, I couldn't afford the expensive medical colleges there. "My father, who was a soldier, died in the India-Pakistan conflict and left us with little."

"My mother... she was always thinking ahead. Before she passed, she'd set up an insurance policy for my education. That money got me into a modest MBBS program in Chennai."

When I arrived at college, I was unprepared for the storm of socializing that awaited me. Other students navigated relationships effortlessly, their easy laughter and casual touches a language I couldn't grasp.

The worn pages of my book offered little comfort as I sat in the classroom, surrounded by the chatter of my classmates. It was only the second day of college, but already I felt like an outsider, a stranger in a foreign land.

Rain tapped on the windows while my friends, sharing stories of past loves and teenage romances, their laughter echoing through the room.

I listened mutely, my experiences world apart from their carefree memories. Love had never been a part of my life, not they described it. My uncle had drilled into me that love wasn't my concern - only studies mattered.

"Hey, Ajith," one of my friends called out, breaking me out of my reverie. "Are you living in some kind of imaginary world or something?"

I forced a smile, but it felt hollow. "I think so," I replied, my gaze drifting around the classroom.

That's when I saw her.

She was standing by the window, washing her hands with water from a bottle. I watched, transfixed, as she took a sipped, the water trickling down through her slim neck. A gentle breeze from the window played with her hair, tousling it softly.

"Hey, Nilu!" someone called from the other side of the room. "I'm coming!" she replied, her voice like music to my ears.

Our eyes met and my heart skipped a beat. Her eyes were mesmerizing, so deep and captivating that I felt as though I could drown in them. Everything faded away.

My pulse raced as she walked past me, a sweet, intoxicating scent trailing in her wake. I closed my eyes, trying to steady myself, but it was no use. I was lost in a haze of emotions I had never experienced before, a whirlwind of sensations that left me breathless and dizzy.

As she moved away, the spell was broken, and I found myself again in the bustling classroom, my friends' voices echoing around me. But the memory of her lingered, a spark of warmth in the otherwise dreary landscape of my life.

I was lost in a world of my own, captivated by the memory of Nilu's smile. The classroom faded into the background, and all I could see was her face, etched into my mind like a beautiful painting.

My friends tried to engage me in conversation, but their words fell on deaf ears. I nodded and smiled, but my thoughts were far away, lost in the depths of Nilu's mesmerizing eyes. Even as I ate my lunch, I barely tasted the food, my appetite diminished by the all-consuming desire to see her again.

As the lunch break ended, a sense of dread washed over me. The prospect of not seeing Nilu again today felt unbearable. I dragged my feet as I made my way to the anatomy labs, my heart heavy with longing.

But entering the lab, my breath caught. There stood Nilu. She looked up as I walked in, and our eyes met again. A smile played on her lips, and I felt my heart soar.

I made my way over to her, my steps tentative and unsure. As I drew closer, I could see how the light danced in her eyes, and how her hair fell softly around her face. She was a vision of beauty, and I was utterly enchanted.

"Hi," I managed to say, my voice barely above a whisper.

"Hi," she replied, her smile widening. "I'm Nilu."

"I'm Ajith," I said, my heart racing as I spoke her name.

We stood there for a moment, lost in each other's gaze. The world faded away as we connected, filling my chest with an unfamiliar warmth.

Working in the lab, our hands brushed as we reached for tools. Each touch sparked electricity through me, making me yearn for more.

"Ajith," my teacher called out, his voice cutting through the murmur of my classmates. "From now on, Nilu will be your lab mate."

My breath caught in my throat as I turned to see Nilu standing beside me, her eyes sparkling with mischief. She flashed me a smile, and my cheeks flushed with heat.

The teacher began his demonstration, explaining the blood test process. I tried to focus on his words, but my mind kept drifted to the girl beside me, the way her hair cascaded over her shoulders, the way her fingers drummed lightly on the lab bench.

"Now," the teacher said, handing Nilu a blood lancet, "pierce your finger and we'll begin the blood test."

I watched, transfixed, as Nilu raised the lancet to her delicate finger. The thought of that sharp point piercing her skin made my stomach churn, and I felt a wave of dizziness wash over me.

"Hey," Nilu said, turning to me with a grin, "I can't do it. Can you do it on my hand?"

She offered her palm and I stared, my mouth dry. The thought of touching her skin made my head spin.

"It's okay," she said softly, her eyes locked.

I took the lancet with shaky hands, almost dropping it when our fingers touched.

Nilu's hand was warm and smooth beneath mine, and I could feel the steady pulse of her heartbeat. I raised the lancet, my breath coming in short, shallow gasps, and pressed it gently against her skin.

But as I did, a sudden wave of dizziness crashed over me. The room tilted and spun, and my knees buckle beneath me. I stumbled, the lancet clattering to the floor, and collapsed in a heap.

Dimly, I heard the teacher's voice, calm and reassuring. "It's okay to be afraid of blood," he said. "It's your first time, isn't it?"

But his words were drowned out by the laughter of my classmates, their mocking tones ringing in my ears. And above it all, I heard Nilu's laughter, bright and clear, like the tinkling of bells.

I felt a hand on my shoulder, and looked up to see my friend standing over me with a glass of lemon juice in his hand. "This will help with the dizziness."

I took a swallow of the drink. Looking up, I saw Nilu watching me, eyes bright with amusement.

"You're funny," she said, her lips curving into a smile.

I felt my face burn with embarrassment, but her smile made it all worth it. I'd made a fool of myself and my classmates laughed, but I'd made her smile - and that was enough.

As the days turned into weeks and the weeks into months, I was drawn to Nilu like a butterfly to a flower. I woke with fresh determination each morning, plotting ways to make her laugh. I practiced jokes in the mirror, perfecting every gesture and word.

Yet, face-to-face, my rehearsed lines vanished. I stumbled over words while her smile and sparkling eyes left me tongue-tied, my heart hammering so loud I thought she must hear it.

Despite my clumsy jokes, Nilu found me endearing. Her melodic laugh filled my chest with warmth - a feeling better than any grade.

Mid-joke about a duck and cook, Nilu's hand touched my shoulder. Her touch jolted through me as my face flushed red.

"I like you, Ajith," she said, her voice soft and sincere. "You're so nice. Do you like me as a friend?"

I tried to speak, but couldn't. My mind spun, processing that Nilu, my dream girl, liked me. As a friend, sure, but it was a start.

"You're so cute, Ajith," she added, her eyes twinkling with mischief.

That was the final straw. My heart began to race, beating so fast I thought it might burst out of my chest. The room started to spin, and I could feel my knees growing weak. Before I knew it, I was falling, my body crumpling to the floor in a heap.

As I lay there, my vision swimming and my ears ringing, I could hear Nilu's laughter above me. It was a sweet sound, tinged with concern.

I felt a splash of cold water hit my face, jolting me back to consciousness. As I blinked rapidly, trying to clear the haze from my vision, I realized my head was resting on something soft and warm. Nilu's face came into focus inches away, worry etched on her delicate features.

"Wake up, Ajith," she said, her voice like velvet caressing my senses. I felt her hand on my cheek, gently wiping away the droplets of water with a towel that bore the faint traces of her lipstick. Her perfume surrounded me, making my heart race again.

"I think he has some serious condition with his brain," one of Nilu's friends chimed in, her voice laced with concern.

Before I could respond, Nilu poured the rest of the water over her friend's head, eliciting a startled yelp. "Shut up," she said, her eyes never leaving mine. "How can I tell her my condition was not brain but my heart when she touches me?" I thought to myself, my cheeks burning with embarrassment.

As the days passed, I became increasingly drawn to Nilu's presence, yet terrified of her effect on me. Her mere touch sent my heart racing and my palms sweating. I tried my best to keep my distance, avoiding any situation where we might make physical contact, but it was a constant struggle.

*****

## Annual day.

The days drifted by in a haze, the years blurring together until Ajith could scarcely remember a time before Nilu had captivated his heart. As the annual day approached, the students were divided into various houses - blue, red, and yellow. And Ajith found himself longing to be on the same team as Nilu.

The yellow house captain called Ajith out, assigning him to play the tableau due to his lack of dancing skills. He nodded, his mind wandering to the classroom where Nilu sat, yearning to see her during the break. The meeting seemed pointless, his thoughts consumed by her presence.

As Ajith approached the classroom, he saw Nilu and her friends laughing together. She walked up to him, her expression growing serious. "Ajith, do you know something?" she asked, her voice low. "Promise me you won't tell anyone about it."

Nilu continued with a hint of excitement in her voice. "When you were outside, the Red House captain came to us." She smiled gently, her eyes sparkling. "Yes, I'm in the Red House."

Her friends giggled, teasing her. "Do you know the captain of the Red House?" they asked, their voices filled with admiration. "They say he's a handsome man with a beard and an incredible physique. His perfume is intoxicating, and his style is so sexy."

Nilu's cheeks flushed as her friends continued to gush about the Red House captain. "He came to our class earlier," one of them said, her voice dreamy. "I felt butterflies in my belly just looking at him."

Another friend sighed, pouting. "But just our bad luck, he's the captain of Nilu's team."

I watched as Nilu pulled me aside, her usual confidence wavering. She guided me to a quiet classroom corner, away from the chatter. Her fingers toyed with her dress hem - a habit I'd grown familiar with.

"There's something I need to tell you," she whispered, her cheeks flushing pink. The sun caught the slight tremor in her hands. "About the Red House captain."

Her voice dropped even lower, forcing me to lean closer. "When I first saw him... his presence was overwhelming. The way he called out to people was so self-assured. I just..." She paused, chewing her lip. "I walked up to him and smiled, but he didn't notice me."

The disappointment in her voice made my chest tighten. She continued, her eyes fixed on the floor. "Later, I overheard some girls talking. Neenu was asking about him, and Sitha..." Nilu's voice caught. "Sitha told her his name - Rudhir."

The way she said his name made my stomach drop. Her eyes took on a dreamy quality I'd never seen before.

"When I heard it, something just clicked in my mind. Rudhir. I thought... I wanted..." She wrapped her arms around herself, lost in the memory. "Then he actually spoke to me and asked for my name. I was so nervous that I blurted out 'Rudhir ' instead of my name."

Her face burned crimson at the memory. "I wanted to disappear right then. Just sink into the ground and vanish." She pressed her palms against her cheeks, trying to cool them. "I've never been so embarrassed in my life."

## When Cupid Misses His Mark

My heart sank as Nilu gushed about Rudhir, the Red House captain. Each word she spoke felt like a dagger twisting in my chest, but I forced a smile, not wanting to betray my true feelings. I couldn't bear to listen any longer, so I interrupted her, my voice strained.

"Nilu, I'm sorry, but can we talk briefly? I need a moment."

She looked at me, concern etched on her face. "Of course, Ajith. Get some rest, and we'll catch up later. But promise not to tell anyone about this."

I nodded, grateful for her understanding. As she walked away, I felt the tears welling in my eyes. I wanted to cry, to release the pain that had been building up inside me, but I couldn't. I couldn't risk breaking our friendship, the one thing I cherished more than anything.

I stood there, lost in thought, weighing my options. Should I confess my feelings to Nilu, risking everything we had built together? Or should I continue as her friend, watching from the sidelines as she fell for someone else?

The thought of losing her friendship was too much to bear. I had always been alone, never knowing the warmth of a genuine connection until Nilu came into my life. Even if it meant watching her love another, I couldn't imagine a world without her by my side.

I took a deep breath, steeling myself for the path ahead. I would remain her friend, no matter how much it hurt. I would be there for her, supporting her through every triumph and heartbreak. Even if my heart, I would endure it, just to see her smile.

*****

I listened to Nilu's stories about Rudhir daily; my heart was sank with every word. They were becoming friends, dancing together at the annual day celebration. I watched from the sidelines, a fake smile on my face as they twirled and laughed.

"Ajith, you won't believe how amazing Rudhir is," Nilu gushed, her eyes sparkling with admiration. "He's so talented and charming. I feel like I can talk to him about anything."

I nodded, swallowing the lump in my throat. "That's great, Nilu. I'm happy for you." The words tasted bitter, but I forced them out, knowing that her happiness was all that mattered.

*****

As I watched Nilu's growing infatuation with Rudhir, a deep sense of loneliness crept into my heart. She was the only girl I had ever truly connected with, the only one who had made me feel like I belonged. But now, as she drifted further away from me, I felt like a lost soul, adrift in a sea of isolation.

In class, I would still talk to Nilu, trying to maintain the friendship we had built. But the moment I stepped into my room at the hostel, the weight of my loneliness would come crashing down upon me. I would bury my face in my pillow, my body wracked with sobs as  I mourned the loss of the only person who had ever made me feel alive.

As the days turned into weeks, the distance between Nilu and me grew ever wider. Where once she would greet me with a cheerful "Good morning!" text, now my inbox remained empty, a silent reminder of the void she had left in my life. On the rare occasions when I mustered the courage to reach out to her, her replies were brief and distant, a mere "Hi" in the evening that felt l i k e  a knife to my heart.

In class, I retreated into my shell, the nerdy introvert who had never dared to speak to anyone. I watched as my classmates laughed and chatted, their easy camaraderie a stark contrast to the loneliness that consumed me. I had been at this college for a year now, but I had never made an effort to connect with anyone beyond Nilu. She had been my world, the only person I had ever let into my heart.

Now, as I sat alone in the cafeteria, picking at my food with disinterest, I realized just how much I had relied on her. Without her, I was lost, a ghost drifting through the halls of the college, invisible to everyone around me. I had never felt so alone, so utterly disconnected from the world around me.

*****

While attending my class one day, my eyes drifted to Nilu`s seat on her bench. And that's when I saw a single tear glistening on her cheek. My heart stopped, my breath caught in my throat. I watched as she wiped it away, her shoulders slumped in defeat.

Before I knew what I was doing, I was on my feet, moving towards her. My own eyes were brimming with tears, my vision blurry as I approached her. She looked up at me, her eyes widening in surprise.

"Ajith, why are you crying?" she asked, her voice soft and concerned.

I shook my head, my tears spilling over. "Why were you crying, you stupid?" I asked, my voice cracking. "I can't handle it when someone cries."

Nilu looked at me, her eyes searching mine. "Is it someone or me?"

We both smiled then, a gentle, sad smile that spoke of our pain. Tears streamed down our faces.

"Can you sit with me today?" Nilu asked, her voice barely above a whisper. "I want you to listen as I want to pour my half of pain into you."

My heart was beating slowly, my eyes still pouring with water. I nodded, unable to speak. I would do anything for her to take away the sadness that seemed to consume her.

I sat down beside Nilu, my heart heavy with concern. She took a deep breath, her eyes still glistening with unshed tears.

"Ajith, I need to tell you about what happened last weekend," she began, her voice trembling slightly. "On Saturday and Sunday, Rudhir and I went out together."

I nodded, my throat tightening.

Nilu looked down at her hands, her fingers twisting together nervously.

She paused, taking a shaky breath. I reached out, placing my hand over hers in a gesture of comfort. She looked up at me, her eyes filled with a pain that I couldn't quite understand.

"I'll tell you what happened," she whispered, her voice barely audible over the pounding of my own heart.

"I was with Rudhir and my friends, which included Niharika," Nilu began, her voice wavering slightly. "We went out together, just hanging out and having fun."

She paused, her eyes distant as if reliving the memories. I swallowed hard, trying to push down the jealousy that threatened to consume me.

"What happened?" I asked softly, my voice barely above a whisper.

Nilu's voice trembled as she continued her story, tears streaming down her face. My heart ached to see her in such pain, and I struggled to keep my own emotions in check.

"We were at the club, dancing and having fun," Nilu said, her voice barely audible over the pounding music in my memory. "Rudhir and Niharika were inseparable, their bodies moving in sync to the beat. I tried to join in, to lose myself in the moment, but I couldn't shake the feeling of being an outsider."

"After the club, Rudhir suggested we go for a drive," Nilu continued, her eyes distant as if reliving the memory. "We ended up on a hill overlooking the city, the stars shining above us. It was beautiful, but..."

She trailed off, her bottom lip quivering. I squeezed her hand, silently urging her to continue.

"That's when they told me," Nilu whispered, her voice cracking. "Rudhir and Niharika, they're together now. A couple."

"I tried to be happy for them," Nilu said, her tears falling faster. "I smiled and congratulated them, but I was falling apart inside. The drive back to the city was unbearable, the silence suffocating. I wanted to scream, to cry, to do something, but I just sat there, numb."

"Thank you, Ajith," she said softly, her voice hoarse from crying. "For being here, for listening. I don't know what I would do without you."

I managed a small smile, even as my own heart ached. "I'll always be here for you, Nilu. No matter what."

And I meant it with every fiber of my being. Even if she never loved me the way I loved her, I would always be there for her, a shoulder to cry on, a friend to lean on. Because that's what love is - putting someone else's happiness before your own, even if it means sacrificing your own heart in the process.

The days that followed were a blur of emotions. Seeing Nilu so heartbroken tore me apart, but a small, selfish part of me couldn't help but feel a glimmer of hope. With Rudhir out of the picture, it felt like Nilu was mine again, like we could go back to the way things were before.

As we spent more time together, our friendship grew stronger than ever. We laughed, we cried, we shared our deepest secrets and fears. I thanked God every day for bringing Nilu back into my life, for giving me another chance to be there for her when she needed me most.

Each day drew me closer to Nilu. Her presence brought a warmth I'd never known. In quiet moments, I'd imagine our future together.

*****

# Bus Ride.

One afternoon, I lazily swirled my coffee as Nilu rambled animatedly beside me in the university cafeteria. Her laughter was infectious, filling the air with a warmth that seemed to chase away the winter morning's chill. I couldn't help but steal glances at her, my heart swelling with affection every time her eyes crinkled joyfully.

A phone call interrupted us. Nilu frowned at the screen before stepping outside to answer.

I watched her through the canteen's windows, her body language shifting from relaxed to tense as the conversation progressed. My stomach twisted with concern as I saw her free hand come up to cover her mouth, her shoulders beginning to shake with what I could only assume were sobs.

Without a second thought, I rushed outside, heart pounding. Nilu turned to me, tears streaming down her face.

"Ajith..." she choked out, her voice thick with emotion.

I didn't hesitate. I murmured soothing words, rubbing her back gently as I tried to comfort her.

After what felt like an eternity, Nilu's sobs began to subside. She pulled back, her eyes red and swollen, and looked up at me with a heartbreaking vulnerability.

"It's my grandmother," she whispered, her voice strained. "She's in the hospital, and... and she's not doing well."

Her words made my heart ache. I knew how much her grandmother meant to her – she had taught Nilu Malayalam, the language of their hometown. She had been a constant presence in Nilu's life, a source of love and support when her parents were busy with work.

"She wants to see me," Nilu continued, her bottom lip trembling. "She said she wants to see me get married before..."

She didn't need to finish the sentence. The implication hung heavy between us, threatening to crush us both.

Without hesitation, I took Nilu's hand in mine, giving it a gentle squeeze.

"We'll go," I said, my voice firm with resolve. "We'll go see her, right away."

Nilu's eyes widened, a flicker of hope sparking to life amidst the sorrow.

"But how?" she asked, her voice laced with desperation. "There are no trains or flights available on such short notice."

I paused, thinking quickly. There had to be a way, some mode of transportation that could get us to Kerala in time.

Then, it hit me.

"The sleeper bus," I said, squeezing Nilu's hand again. "It's not ideal, but it'll get us there by morning if we leave now."

Nilu's face crumpled with relief, and she threw her arms around me, holding me tight.

"Thank you," she whispered, her voice thick with emotion. "Thank you for being here and willing to do this for me."

"I'll check the bus schedules," I said, pulling out my phone with trembling fingers. "I can take leave from college too. You shouldn't travel alone at a time like this."

Fresh tears spilled down Nilu's cheeks. "I'll travel any way possible. I just need to get to her."

I swallowed hard as I scrolled through the bus options, my face heating up. "It's... It's a sleeper bus though..." I said, unable to meet Nilu's eyes. "And the only seats available are in the double bed cabin."

My heart raced at the implication. Sharing such an intimate space with Nilu, even if just for travel? The thought made my palms sweat. But one look at her tear-stained face steeled my resolve.

"If you're okay with that, I mean," I added quickly. "We can look for other options too..."

"Ajith," Nilu cut me off, wiping her eyes. "You're my best friend. There's nothing to worry about. We can keep our distance during the night journey." She placed her hand on my arm. "I actually feel safer with you around."

I completed the transaction, but my fingers were still shaking slightly. The confirmation message popped up on my screen - two tickets for the long-distance trip from Chennai to Kerala that would take us through the night.

"Done," I said softly. "We leave at eleven tonight."

Nilu squeezed my arm again, her touch sending warmth through my entire body. "Thank you, Ajith. I don't know what I'd do without you."

I finally looked up at her. Her eyes were still red from crying, but gratitude and relief written across her face.

I stood with Nilu outside the small roadside shop, our bags at our feet. The night air was thick with humidity, and the occasional car headlights swept across us as we waited.

The bus pulled up just after midnight. We climbed aboard, making our way to our assigned berth on the upper level. The purple fluorescent lights cast a soft glow across the narrow space, and a beige curtain hung ready to provide privacy from the other passengers.

I climbed onto the bed, pressing myself against the window to give Nilu as much space as possible. The driver had handed me a water bottle earlier, which I placed between us like an awkward barrier.

Nilu's eyes were still puffy from crying. She lay on her side, facing me, her hair splayed across the pillow.

"Try not to worry too much," I whispered, keeping my voice low to avoid disturbing the other passengers. "We'll be there by morning."

She nodded, but her lower lip trembled. "I can't sleep, Ajith. My mind won't stop racing. Could we... could we just talk for a while?"

"Of course," I said, adjusting my position to face her better. The water bottle rolled slightly between us as the bus swayed. "I'm here to listen."

Nilu drew in a shaky breath, her fingers fidgeting with the edge of the blanket. "Thank you. I really need someone to talk to right now."

She paused for a moment, gathering her thoughts, then began to speak.

Nilu drew in a deep breath, her fingers fidgeting with the edge of the blanket. "Ajith, I don't want to get married now. I like to have a guy like Rudhir who can take me anywhere, give me that vibe. I don't want to be trapped as a housewife. I want freedom to travel and pursue my acting dreams."

She paused, her eyes searching mine. "I wish I could have had Rudhir."

I felt a pang at her words, but pushed it aside. "Rudhir's not a good guy, Nilu," I said gently. "You deserve someone better than him."

Nilu sighed. "I know, but he's like that after his parents divorced. It really affected him."

Nodding slowly, I met her gaze. "If you marry someone random, you might not get the life you want. The freedom, the travel, the acting."

Nilu's eyes widened slightly. "How would you treat your wife then, Ajith?"

My heart raced as I formed the words carefully. "A wife isn't property. She's her own person who deserves to chase her dreams and make her own choices. Why should she need permission from anyone?"

Nilu's eyes locked with mine in the dim light of the bus.

"Marriage should be a partnership," I continued, my voice soft but firm. "Like best friends, but deeper. Two people supporting each other's growth, understanding each other's thoughts without words."

"That's... different from what most guys think," Nilu whispered.

I swallowed hard. "If I had a wife who loved acting, I'd be at every premiere. I'd go with her or wish her amazing adventures if she wanted to travel. Her happiness would be my happiness."

The bus swayed gently as we discussed life, love, and dreams. Nilu shared her fears about societal expectations, and I listened, offering perspectives that challenged traditional views.

"It's about growing together," I said, knowing in my heart I would do anything to support her dreams, even if she never saw me as more than a friend. "Each person should lift the other higher."

"I wish more men thought like you," Nilu murmured, her eyes growing heavy with sleep.

I watched her drift off, my chest aching with unspoken feelings. I'd give her the moon if she asked, but being her trusted friend was enough. Even if she never chose me, I wanted to be the kind of man who deserved someone like her.

As Nilu drifted deeper into sleep, raindrops began to patter against the bus window. The streetlights we passed cast fleeting golden halos across her face, illuminating her face in an ethereal glow. The purple curtain behind her billowed softly in the cold air from the AC, creating an almost dreamlike atmosphere in our small shared space.

My pulse raced beneath my ribs as I watched her peaceful expression. Her long lashes cast delicate shadows on her cheeks, and a few strands of hair had fallen across her face. Without thinking, I reached out to gently brush them away, my fingers trembling.

"If only you were mine," I whispered, so quietly the words were nearly lost in the sound of rain. The thought of spending my life with her, supporting her dreams, being there for every triumph and setback, made my chest ache with longing.

Before I could stop myself, I leaned forward and pressed the softest kiss to her forehead. Her skin was warm beneath my lips, and she smelled faintly of jasmine. My pulse raced at the intimate gesture, but Nilu didn't stir. The stress of the day and her emotional exhaustion had pulled her into a deep slumber.

I pulled back, watching as she shifted slightly in her sleep, her breathing steady and peaceful. The rain continued its gentle rhythm against the window, creating a cocoon of tranquility around us. In this moment, suspended between night and dawn, I allowed myself to imagine a future where she might feel the same way about me.

I spent the entire night watching Nilu's peaceful face, unable to find sleep myself. The bus lurched and swayed, making frequent stops that prevented any real rest. My bladder protested the lack of bathroom breaks, but I didn't dare move and disturb her slumber.

The sunrise painted Kerala's lush landscape in golden hues as Nilu's phone rang. She jolted awake, her face immediately tensing as she saw her mother's name on the screen.

"Mom?" Her voice cracked with worry.

I held my breath, watching her expression shift from fear to relief. Her shoulders relaxed, and she pressed a hand to her heart.

Grandmother is back home? Thank God.

When we arrived at their house, her grandmother sat propped up on pillows in the living room, frail but smiling.

"You must marry soon, Nilu," her grandmother said, clasping Nilu's hands. "I want to see you as a bride before..."

Nilu's smile faltered. "Grandmother, please don't talk like that."

"We're registering her on a matrimonial site," Nilu's mother announced. "It's time she settled down."

I watched Nilu's face fall, though she tried to hide it behind a weak smile. Later, she found me sitting alone on the veranda.

"Ajith," she whispered, sinking beside me. "I'm scared. Marriage terrifies me. What if I lose myself? What if my dreams die? But I can't break grandmother's heart either." Her eyes filled with tears. "What should I do?"

My heart ached for her distress. She looked to me for answers, trusting me as her closest friend, while I wrestled with my unspoken feelings for her. I knew I had to do something, anything, to help her escape this predicament. And so, I devised a plan.

"Nilu, listen to me," I said, my voice filled with urgency. "Marrying someone you don't know can be dangerous. You have no idea what kind of person they are, what their habits are, or even if they snore like a freight train!"

Nilu couldn't help but giggle at my exaggerated description. "But Ajith, what choice do I have?" she asked, her smile fading.

"You have me," I blurted out, my heart racing. "Marry me instead."

Nilu's eyes widened in shock. "What? But Ajith, we're just friends..."

"I know, I know," I said, my palms sweating. "But think about it. You know me, you trust me. I would never force you to do anything you don't want to do. And besides."

Nilu burst out laughing, her eyes crinkling at the corners. "You're crazy, you know that?" she said, shaking her head.

But as the laughter subsided, a thoughtful expression crossed her face. "You know, maybe you're right," she said slowly. "Maybe marrying someone I already know and trust is the best option."

With a pounding heart, I watched Nilu's expression shift from surprise to contemplation. Could she actually be considering my crazy proposal?

"You're serious?" she asked, eyes searching mine intently.

I took a deep breath and nodded. "Deadly serious. Marry me, Nilu. At least you know I'll never try to control or hold you back from your dreams."

A small smile tugged at the corners of her mouth. "You really would support me pursuing acting, wouldn't you?"

"Of course!" I exclaimed vehemently. "I'll be your biggest fan, front row at every show."

Nilu's smile widened into a grin, and she threw her arms around me in a tight hug. "You're the best friend a girl could ask for, Ajith. I don't know what I'd do without you."

As she pulled back, her eyes shone with gratitude and a hint of something more I dared not name. "Okay, let's do it. Let's get married."

＊＊＊＊＊

# Tying the Knot

After a year of heartfelt preparations and convincing our families, Nilu and I stood hand-in-hand beneath a canopy of fragrant jasmine garlands. Her deep eyes shimmered with unshed tears as the pandit tied our hands with the sacred thread. This was really happening - I was marrying my best friend, the woman I had loved silently for so long.

As we circled the sacred fire, our souls linking with every step, I couldn't help but smile. Nilu caught my eye and smiled back brightly. At that moment, nothing else mattered except the bond we shared.

The grand wedding celebrations sped by in a vibrant blur of music, laughter, and nonstop well-wishes. But through it all, Nilu's hand stayed firmly in mine, serving as an anchor amid the joyful chaos.

And then, it was just the two of us alone at last. My wife. My Nilu. Our life together was only just beginning.

*****

Life as newlyweds was an adventure, to say the least. We quickly discovered that living together was a whole new ballgame, filled with unexpected challenges and hilarious mishaps.

"Ajith, did you use my toothbrush again?" Nilu called out from the bathroom one morning.

"What? No, of course not!" I replied, frantically trying to hide the evidence.

But despite the occasional fight, we were happily content. We learned to understand each other's quirks and routines, and found happiness in the simple joys of home life.

As we settled into our new routine, I couldn't help but reflect on the journey that had brought us here. From the shy, awkward boy who had first laid eyes on Nilu all those years ago, to the man who now shared her life and her heart, I had come a long way.

As I watched Nilu move around our cozy home, her face shining with contentment, I knew I would do anything to keep that smile on her face. Because ultimately, that was all that mattered—being together, facing whatever challenges life brought us, and finding laughter and love along the way.

Inspector Daniel leaned back in his chair, regarding the disheveled man across the table with a mix of skepticism and disdain. Ajith's tale of a lovestruck college student seemed like a fanciful work of fiction, utterly at odds with the evidence before him.

"Enough," Daniel said, raising a hand to silence Ajith mid-sentence. "You spin quite the romantic yarn, I'll give you that. A great writer you would make."

Ajith opened his mouth to protest, but Daniel cut him off sharply. "Save your breath. The man before me is far from the noble, lovesick youth you describe." He gestured at Ajith's unkempt appearance, the stale odor of alcohol clinging to his clothes. "An alcoholic wreck is what I see. A man cruel enough to make his wife and child fear for their lives, according to my investigation."

Tears welled up in Ajith's eyes, but Daniel remained unmoved. "Why are you really an alcoholic, hmm? I find it hard to digest this sappy tale of yours."

Ajith's shoulders slumped in defeat. "I'll explain everything," he whispered, his voice cracking with emotion. "Just let me--"

"No more romance novels for now," Daniel interrupted, his tone flat. "I want the truth and nothing but."

Ajith nodded meekly, fresh tears spilling down his cheeks as Daniel fixed him with an unwavering stare, determined to uncover the real story behind this baffling mystery.

I stared at my reflection in the bathroom mirror during one of Nilu's lavish parties, barely recognizing the man looking back at me.

"Here, try this." One of her co-stars pressed another cocktail into my hand. "Loosen up, doc. You're too stiff."

I knocked it back, the burn in my throat becoming familiar. The faces around me blurred as Nilu's laughter echoed from the next room, surrounded by her adoring fans and fellow actors.

"Your wife's latest film crossed a hundred crores," someone said, clapping my shoulder. "You must be proud."

I forced a smile, but my stomach churned. My hospital salary felt pathetic compared to what she earned in a single movie. I worked double shifts, took extra consultations, anything to prove I could provide for her like those leading men she acted with.

"Have a cigar," another actor offered. "Makes you look sophisticated."

I never smoked before, but I took it. Anything to fit in with her world. The smoke made me cough, but I persisted. Better to look cool than bookish.

Every premiere, every award show, every success party - I drowned myself in liquid courage. Wine wasn't enough anymore. Beer became rum became whiskey. The bottles helped blur the line between the quiet boy and the sophisticated husband Nilu deserved.

"Look at those heroes she works with," I muttered to myself one night, watching her latest film. "I can be better than them. I have to be."

The alcohol made me feel invincible, like I could match their charm and confidence. But in the morning,

I'd wake up hollow, further from myself than ever. Still, I couldn't stop.

Those parties were my undoing. I had to be the man Nilu deserved, someone as cool and confident as the heroes she acted alongside. But the more I drank to fit in, the more I lost myself.

That's how I became this person. I thought drinking would help me measure up, but it only left me hollow and unrecognizable.

One day I need to beat Nilu, I regret it, but the reason is...

"I... I didn't mean to hurt her," I stammered, my voice barely above a whisper. "It was a mistake, a terrible mistake."

I took a deep breath, trying to steady myself. "Nilu... she was angry. Anvi had been playing with her phone, and Nilu lost her temper. She started hitting Anvi, screaming at her. I couldn't bear to see my little girl in pain."

I closed my eyes, the memory of that awful moment flashing through my mind. "I tried to stop her, to pull her away from Anvi. But Nilu... she wouldn't listen. "

I could feel the tears streaming down my face now, hot and heavy. "I... I lost control. I couldn't take it anymore. I grabbed Nilu, tried to shake some sense into her. But she fought back, screaming and clawing at me. And then... then I hit her."

I buried my face in my hands, my shoulders shaking with sobs. "I never meant to hurt her. I loved her more than anything in this world. But seeing her hurting Anvi... it broke something inside of me."

I looked up at the inspector, my eyes pleading for understanding. "I know what I did was wrong. But in that moment, I could only think about protecting my daughter."

I took a shuddering breath, my voice barely audible. "I'm sorry. I'm so sorry. I never wanted any of this to happen. I just... I just wanted to keep my family safe. And now... now I've lost everything."

Chapter 5

# The Unfolding Truth

Inspector Daniel raised his hand, cutting off Ajith's story. His stern facade cracked, revealing the emotional toll of the confession. He leaned forward across the interrogation table.

"I need you to stop." Daniel's voice wavered. "Your story... it's affecting me more than it should. I want to believe you, but the evidence..."

Ajith wiped his reddened eyes with his sleeve. The stench of alcohol still clung to him, but his gaze held a painful clarity.

"All these accusations against you."

"Ajith, I want to believe you. I think you loved Nilu, but I need to know why all this happened.

Before Ajith could utter another word, a knock at the door interrupted them. Sub-Inspector Akhil's urgent voice called out, "Sir, please open the door.

someone sent a video, and he says he has some answers."

Inspector Daniel jumped from his chair, his eyes wide with anticipation. Ajith, crying and heartbroken throughout his story, collapsed before responding to the inspector's question.

Akhil rushed to Ajith's side, checking his pulse. He turned to Daniel, his voice filled with urgency. "Inspector, you need to go to the office. It's important."

Daniel hesitated for a moment, torn between his desire to hear Ajith's response and the potential breakthrough in the case. He glanced at Ajith's unconscious form, then back at Akhil.

"Make sure he gets medical attention," Daniel instructed, his voice strained. "I'll be in the office."

Daniel rushed to the office, where officers huddled around Anvi's mobile screen, eager to see Sentinel's video.

"What do we have?" Daniel demanded, pushing his way to the front.

A figure appeared on the screen, his voice distorted. "Inspector Daniel, I have information that may shed light on the disappearance of Nilu and her daughter."

The room fell silent as everyone leaned in, hanging on Sentinel's every word. Daniel's heart pounded in his chest, hoping that this mysterious figure held the key to unravelling the tragic mystery that had consumed them all.

"He sent it on Anvi's Discord, sir," an officer replied, his eyes glued to the screen. "But we can't trace anything more than the message itself."

Inspector Daniel nodded, his brow furrowed as he focused on the video. Sentinel`s distorted voice continued, drawing everyone's attention.

*****

As the video played, Inspector Daniel leaned forward, his eyes fixed on the screen. Sentinel's distorted voice filled the room, revealing a shocking truth.

"Ajith, Anvi, and Nilu were not a perfect family. A lot was happening behind closed doors that no one knew about."

Daniel's eyes widened, his mind racing with the implications of this revelation.

Sentinel continued, his voice steady and confident. "I had installed cameras in their house, cameras that no one could see. Microphones too. I have recordings of what happened in that house, evidence that will shed light on the truth."

The inspector's heart pounded in his chest, a mix of excitement and disbelief coursing through his veins. How had Sentinel managed to infiltrate the house so thoroughly?

As if reading Daniel's mind, Sentinel addressed his unspoken questions. "You might be wondering why you didn't see any camera. The reason is simple. I wanted to solve the case before you could find them, and I removed them once I had gathered the necessary evidence."

Daniel leaned back, his mind reeling. Despite his investigative pride, Sentinel had outmaneuvered him completely. The mysterious vigilante had pieced together clues in ways Daniel could only dream of.

The video flickered to life, revealing a heart-wrenching scene. Nilu, her face streaked with tears, held the phone to her ear as she poured out her pain.

"Rudhir. He... he hit me because I beat Anvi," Nilu sobbed, her voice trembling. "I lost control. I couldn't even explain that I was texting you on the phone."

On the other end of the line, Rudhir's voice was a soothing balm to her wounded soul. "I'm sorry.

Nilu sniffled, wiping her eyes with the back of her hand. "There is no film shoot tomorrow," she said softly, her voice almost a whisper.

"I'll come over after Ajith and Anvi have left for the day," Rudhir promised, his words a lifeline for Nilu to cling to.

The scene changed, and sunlight poured through Nilu's windows. She waited nervously for Rudhir to arrive, her heart racing.

A sleek white car pulled to the curb, its engine purring like a contented cat. The door swung open, and Rudhir emerged, looking every inch the dashing hero. His crisp white shirt and perfectly tailored trousers accentuated his tall, lean frame, and his dark hair was swept back in a stylish coif.

He held a bouquet of vibrant red roses in his hands, their petals glistening with dew. With a confident stride, he made his way towards Nilu's door, his eyes fixed on his destination.

When he finally stepped through the door, she rushed into his arms, burying her face in his chest as if seeking shelter from the storm of her life.

Rudhir held her tight, his strong arms enveloping her in a cocoon of safety and warmth. He stroked her hair, his touch gentle and comforting. Nilu looked up at him, her eyes shimmering with unshed tears.

"I missed you so much," she whispered, her voice raw with emotion.

Rudhir leaned down, capturing her lips in a tender kiss. Nilu melted into his embrace, savoring the taste of him, the feel of his body pressed against hers. Everything else faded away in that moment- the pain, the heartache, the fear. All that mattered was Rudhir and the love they shared.

As they parted, Nilu gazed up at Rudhir adoringly, her eyes filled with love and desperation. "You make my life perfect," she breathed, clinging to him as if he were her only lifeline.

Rudhir grinned, his eyes sparkling with mischief and desire. "Is a kiss enough? I want to love you so much today that you'll feel like we're in heaven."

Nilu's heart raced at his words, desire coursing through her veins. She wanted nothing more than to lose herself in Rudhir's touch, to forget the pain and heartache of her life with Ajith. In Rudhir's arms, she felt alive, cherished, and loved in a way she had never experienced.

Inspector Daniel's mind raced as he recalled the name Rudhir. He remembered the charming man from her college days, who had captured Nilu's heart. Daniel had always admired Rudhir's charisma and his ability to navigate social situations effortlessly. Still, he wondered if there was more to the man than met the eye.

As he watched the video footage, Daniel couldn't help but feel a twinge of sympathy for Ajith. The poor man had been trapped in a loveless marriage, unaware of his wife's infidelity and the depths of her unhappiness. Daniel could only imagine the pain and betrayal Ajith must have felt when he discovered the truth.

But even as he felt for Ajith, Daniel's thoughts turned to Rudhir and Niharika. He remembered how they had been inseparable in college, the perfect couple everyone envied. What had happened to their relationship?

Inspector Daniel's phone buzzed with another notification. His fingers trembled as he opened the new video from Sentinel, his jaw clenched tight with anticipation.

The footage started playing, most of it heavily pixelated and blurred. Through static and distortion, shapes move in intimate choreography. The inspector's face flushed red as he realized what he was witnessing. His knuckles turned white as he gripped the phone tighter.

The audio came through crystal clear despite the visual censoring. Rudhir's voice dripped with confidence as he pulled Nilu closer, their silhouettes merging in the blurred frame. Daniel shifted uncomfortably in his chair, like an unwilling voyeur to this intimate moment.

His professional detachment wavered as he watched the scene unfold. How Rudhir commanded the space and how Nilu responded to his presence painted a vivid picture of their affair. Daniel's stomach churned with disgust and pity - disgust at the betrayal, pity for the broken home this revealed.

Through gaps in the pixelation, Daniel caught glimpses of Rudhir's sculpted physique as he removed his shirt. The inspector noted how different this Rudhir was from his public persona - the polished political figure transformed into something more primal.

Nilu's breathy sighs filled the audio feed. The raw desire in her voice made Daniel wince. He'd interviewed her fans who spoke of her grace and poise. This recording shattered that image completely.

As the video continued, Daniel's expression shifted from revulsion to pity. He couldn't help but feel sorry for Ajith.

Daniel shook his head, trying to clear his thoughts. He had to remain objective, to focus on the facts of the case. But as he watched Rudhir and Nilu's bodies entwine, he couldn't help but wonder what had driven them to such desperate measures.

The following message from Sentinel was a voice note rather than a video. His distorted voice filled the room, heavy with a mix of disgust and regret.

"I couldn't edit the video footage of what happened next. It was something I couldn't even bear to look at, let alone process."

Daniel's brow furrowed as he listened, his mind racing with the implications of Sentinel's words. What could have been so more disturbing than this?

The voice note crackled to life, Sentinel's distorted voice filling the room with a sense of dread.

"What I witnessed next was truly horrifying."

Anvi clutched her stomach, her face contorted in pain as she approached the front door. The school staff had tried to contact her parents, but to no avail. She had assured them that her mother would be home, as there was no shooting scheduled for the day.

With shaky hands, Anvi retrieved the spare key from her pocket and unlocked the door. As she stepped inside, a strange noise caught her attention. It sounded like muffled voices coming from her parents' bedroom.

Curiosity got the better of her, and despite the pain in her stomach, Anvi crept towards the room. As she drew closer, the voices became clearer, and she recognized her mother's voice, along with a man's voice that definitely didn't belong to her father.

Anvi's heart raced as she reached for the doorknob, her hand trembling. She hesitated for a moment, unsure if she really wanted to know what was happening behind that door. But the need for answers overpowered her fear, and she slowly turned the knob.

The door swung open, revealing a sight that made Anvi's blood run cold. There, on the bed, was her mother, wrapped in the arms of a man she had never seen before. They were both naked, their bodies intertwined in a passionate embrace.

Anvi gasped, the sound alerting the lovers to her presence. Nilu's eyes widened in shock and horror as she saw her daughter standing in the doorway. She quickly pulled the sheets up to cover herself, but it was too late. Anvi had seen everything.

"Anvi!" Nilu exclaimed, her voice trembling. "What are you doing home?"

But Anvi couldn't speak. She stood there, frozen, her mind reeling from the betrayal she had just witnessed. Tears welled up in her eyes as she stared at her mother, the woman she had always looked up to and admired.

Rudhir's heart raced as he watched the young girl stumble through the doorway, her eyes wide with shock and betrayal. He cursed under his breath, rushing towards her in a desperate attempt to keep her quiet.

"Anvi, wait!" Nilu cried, her voice trembling with fear. "Please, let me explain."

But Anvi was inconsolable, tears streaming down her face as she backed away from Rudhir's advancing figure. In her panic, she tripped and fell down the stairs, hitting her head on the floor with a sickening crack.

Rudhir froze, staring at the motionless girl in horror. Nilu let out a strangled sob, rushing to her daughter's side. "Anvi! Oh god, what have we done?"

Thinking quickly, Rudhir tore off the nearest piece of clothing - Anvi's dress - and began wiping the blood from the floor. Nilu watched in stunned silence as he efficiently cleaned the scene, his movements calm and calculated.

Rudhir placed his hands on Nilu's shoulders. "Quick—change her clothes and toss them in the washing machine."

Nilu changed her bloody clothes for clean ones.

"We need to get her out of here," Rudhir said, his voice low and urgent. "The hospital is too risky - they'll ask questions." He turned to Nilu, his dark eyes narrowed. ". We're leaving."

Nilu hesitated, her gaze darting between her unconscious daughter and the man who had so callously taken charge. "But Anvi-"

"Is collateral damage," Rudhir snapped, his patience wearing thin. "We can't afford to let her ruin everything." He scooped up the girl's limp form, ignoring Nilu's anguished cries. "Now move before someone comes looking."

Nilu's world shattered as she watched Rudhir handle her daughter's body with such cold detachment. The man she had moments ago embraced now appeared as a stranger, his handsome features twisted into something monstrous.

"No!" She lunged at him, her fists pounding against his chest. "Let her go! We need to get her help!"

Rudhir caught her wrists in one hand, his grip like iron. With his free hand, he pulled a gun from his discarded jacket and pressed it against Anvi's temple. The metal gleamed in the afternoon light.

"Get in the car, Nilu." His voice held none of the warmth she had once found so captivating. "Now."

"Please," she sobbed, her knees buckling. "She's my baby. My little girl."

"Your little girl who just saw too much." He jerked his head toward the door. "The car. Don't make me say it again."

Nilu's tears fell freely as she stared at the weapon pressed against her daughter's head. The perfect features she had once traced with loving fingers now seemed harsh and cruel. Her stomach churned at the memory of their passionate embrace just minutes ago.

"You're a monster," she whispered, backing away from him.

"Maybe." He shrugged, unmoved by her words. "But I'm a monster with a gun pointed at your daughter's head. Move."

Nilu stumbled toward the door, her legs barely supporting her weight. Each step felt like walking through quicksand as she made her way to his white car, now transformed from a chariot of passion into a vessel of nightmares.

She slid into the passenger seat, her body wracked with sobs. Through tear-blurred vision, she watched as Rudhir carefully arranged Anvi's unconscious form in the backseat, the gun never wavering from its target.

Daniel stared at the screen, his heart pounding in his chest as he listened to Sentinel's chilling account.

He clenched his fists, anger coursing through his veins. How could Rudhir be so selfish, so callous? They had put his own desires above the well-being of an innocent child, and now Anvi was paying the price.

Daniel's mind raced with the implications of this new information. If Rudhir and Nilu had indeed fled with Anvi's unconscious body, then the case had just taken a dark and disturbing turn. He couldn't even begin to imagine the horrors the poor girl might be enduring at their hands.

Guilt washed over Daniel as he processed the revelations. He should have noticed sooner and investigated more thoroughly. His lack of diligence might have allowed this tragedy to unfold.

Self-pity could wait. Daniel needed to act quickly to rescue Anvi and catch her kidnappers. He couldn't let emotions cloud his judgment.

Taking a deep breath, he pushed aside his feelings to focus on the task. He stood from his desk, vowing to find Anvi and put Rudhir behind bars, no matter the cost.

Chapter 6

# Breaking Point

## A Year ago

Ajith groaned, clutching his abdomen as a sharp pain lanced through his gut. He stumbled down the hospital corridor, desperate to find Dr. Pranav.

"Pranav!" he gasped, entering the gastroenterologist's office. "Something's wrong..."

Pranav leaped to his feet, steadying his friend. "What is it? Talk to me."

"My stomach..." Ajith grimaced, doubling over. "It feels like I'm being stabbed through."

Pranav pulled out his stethoscope, his brow furrowed. "How much have you been drinking lately?"

"Same as usual." Ajith slumped into a chair, his face pale and clammy.

"And the smoking? You know these habits wreak havoc on your digestive system."

"I need an honest assessment." Ajith's voice cracked.

Pranav helped Ajith onto the examination table, his movements careful and deliberate. "We need to do an endoscopy first thing tomorrow morning. This pain isn't normal, and I want to get a clear look inside."

"Tomorrow?".

"You need to fast for at least eight hours before the procedure. Go home, don't eat anything after midnight." Pranav scribbled on his prescription pad. "Take these for the pain tonight."

The following day, Pranav's worried face hovered above him.

"Just relax," Pranav said, inserting the endoscope's thin tube down Ajith's throat. "Try to breathe normally."

Ajith gagged as the camera snaked its way through his esophagus and into his stomach. Pranav studied the images intently on the monitor, guiding the scope deeper.

Later, Pranav sat holding the endoscopy images, his face grim. He tapped one frame with a pen.

"I found multiple lesions," Pranav said, his voice tight. "The biopsy will confirm it, but..." He spread the endoscopy images across the blanket. "These dark patches here and here - they're consistent with gastric carcinoma."

Ajith stared at the images, his mouth dry. "Cancer?"

"Stage two, from what I can see." Pranav gripped Ajith's shoulder. "We'll start treatment immediately. I've already contacted the oncology department."

"Does this explain the pain?"

"The location of the tumors..." Pranav pointed to the images. "They're pressing against nerve clusters. That's what's causing your symptoms."

Ajith closed his eyes, his head swimming with more than just the lingering effects of anesthesia. All those nights, he'd blamed the alcohol for his stomach pain, all those mornings, he'd convinced himself it was just another hangover.

"Save the lecture." Ajith turned away.

"Treatment options exist, but..." Pranav's voice trailed off.

Ajith reached for his phone, thumb hovering over Nilu's number. He paused. Let them think it's just the drinking, he thought—the weakness, the pain - they'd attribute it all to his vices—better that way.

"Don't tell Nilu or Anvi." Ajith's eyes locked with Pranav's.

"Promise me."

"But they're your loved ones-" Pranav protested to Ajith.

"Promise me."

Pranav nodded reluctantly.

Ajith stumbled to his car, prescription in hand. At a pharmacy far from home, he bought the medications, tucking them under his seat. Before reaching home, he pulled out a bottle of whiskey, splashing it over his clothes and swishing it in his mouth. better they believe I was intoxicated rather than ill.

The drive home stretched endlessly. His knuckles whitened on the steering wheel as thoughts crashed through his mind - the cancer eating away at him, Nilu's worried face, Anvi's innocent smile. How long could he keep up this charade? The medicine rattled in its hiding place, a constant reminder of the secret he now carried.

Ajith stumbled up the steps as the late sun cast shadows, his clothes stinking of whiskey. The door creaked open, revealing Anvi's tiny face, peering up at him.

"Dad?" Her voice quivered. "Why are you drinking on Mom's birthday?"

The words hit him like a physical blow. Birthday. Nilu's birthday. How could he have forgotten?

Through the doorway, he saw the living room transformed - streamers hung from the ceiling, balloons floated in the corners, and a pile of wrapped presents covered the coffee table. Nilu stood among a group of well-dressed friends, her smile wavering as she saw him.

"Look who finally showed up," one of her friends muttered.

A different guest moved closer, arms crossed. "We've been waiting to see your big surprise, Ajith. Where's the flowers? What present did you get her?

Ajith's hands hung empty at his sides. The room spun slightly as guilt crashed over him.

Tears welled in Nilu's eyes. "Is this really how you want me to spend my special day?"

"No tears, honey." Her friends gathered close to comfort her. "We're here for you, aren't we?"

A well-dressed man—one of Nilu's co-stars—grabbed Ajith's arm and guided him toward the door. "What's wrong with you? Making her cry on her birthday?" His voice lowered to a harsh whisper. "You're ruining everything."

Ajith caught one last glimpse of the scene - Nilu dabbing her eyes while friends consoled her, Anvi watching with confusion and hurt, the cheerful decorations now seeming to mock his failure. The door closed behind him with a final click.

Ajith's car swerved through empty streets, tears blurring his vision. His hands shook on the steering wheel as memories flooded back - Nilu's disappointed face, Anvi's confusion, the disease devouring him from within. He pulled over, unable to drive through the storm of emotions.

Inside the house, Nilu collapsed onto the couch after her friends departed. Anvi curled up beside her, small fingers clutching her mother's sleeve.

"How come Daddy's not the same anymore?" Anvi asked, her voice trembling.

Nilu stroked her daughter's hair, fighting back fresh tears. "I don't know I don't know."

Miles away, Ajith's fist slammed against his steering wheel. Sobs wracked his body as he hunched over, the pain in his stomach mixing with the agony in his heart. Empty bottles rattled in the backseat - his shield, his excuse, his way to hide the truth.

"I'm sorry," he choked out to the empty car. "I'm so sorry."

In his car, Ajith clutched his stomach as another wave of pain hit. He fumbled for his hidden pills, swallowing them dry. The prescription bottle mocked him - a countdown to an ending he couldn't share. His wedding ring caught the streetlight, sending fresh waves of grief through him.

"I can't tell them," he whispered, voice raw. "I can't watch them suffer through this too."

The following days blurred together in a haze of tension and unspoken pain. Ajith and Nilu drifted apart like ships passing in the night, their once warm embraces replaced by strained silences.

Ajith fully committed to his deception, staggering into the house at irregular times with alcohol on his breath. He muttered profanities, slammed doors shut, and hurled glass containers until they shattered against the surface whenever Nilu tried to approach. Part of him hoped the drunken monster act would make it easier if... when the end came.

"Maybe they won't grieve as hard for the town drunk," he muttered.

Anvi tiptoed around him, eyes downcast whenever he erupted in towering rages over imagined slights. Nilu simply retreated, lips pressed into a tight line, tears glistening in the corners of her eyes when she thought no one could see.

In secret moments, Ajith poured over investment portfolios and bank statements, meticulously shifting funds into accounts under Anvi's name. He scoured the internet for the perfect gift - something to make up for the lost moments, all the pain he was causing.

A high-end gaming laptop, top of the line, arrived in an unmarked box. He hid it under a tarp in the garage until Anvi's birthday. When the day came, he thrust the heavy package into her hands, his words more bark than speech.

"Here. For your grades. Make sure you get into a good college."

Anvi's eyes widened at the shiny laptop. She looked up at her father with longing, hesitation flickering across her face. Slowly and carefully, she wrapped her arms around him in a hug.

Ajith stiffened, then shoved her away, the tender gesture too much for his fracturing heart to bear. "Don't get sappy! Just take it and go study!"

Anvi stumbled back, cradling the laptop against her chest as tears sprang to her eyes. She nodded jerkily and fled to her room, the sound of her muffled sobs trailing after her.

Nilu walked out of the kitchen, her face set in a grim line. "Was that really necessary?"

Ajith shrugged, feigning indifference as his insides twisted with self-loathing. "She needs to toughen up."

"She's just a child!"

"Well, maybe if her mother were around more often-"

The crack of Nilu's palm across his cheek cut him off. She glared at him through furious tears, then whirled and stormed away, leaving a ringing silence in her wake.

The days stretched into weeks in that hollow house. Anvi remained locked in her room, the whirr of the laptop's fan her only company. Nilu worked endless hours on set, coming home well past midnight and rising again before dawn.

Ajith drifted through the empty spaces like a ghost, choking down medication in solitary rituals. Hollow-eyed, he studied the faces around him - Nilu's withdrawn weariness, Anvi's despondent silence - and felt perversely satisfied.

"Better this way," he rasped into the bottom of a bottle one night. "Better they think of me with hatred than with pity."

The house became a mausoleum, joy buried deep. When voices broke the silence, they cut like knives - harsh shouts and bitter accusations. Every interaction bore the weight of the secret eating at Ajith's core.

Time slipped away, indistinguishable day from night, smile from sneer, love from loathing. Only the dwindling supply of Ajith's medication marked the inexorable march toward an ending none could see approaching.

One night, Ajith lurched home past midnight, whiskey-soaked. The house was dark except for kitchen light, his steps echoing as memories rushed in.

Years ago, they would sit together at that same wooden table, shoulders touching as they shared meals. Nilu would tear pieces of chapati, dip them in curry, and feed him with her delicate fingers. Her eyes would crinkle with joy whenever he praised her cooking.

Tonight, like most nights, a plate sat abandoned on the dining table. Half-eaten chapatis lay scattered beside unwashed dishes, unlike Nilu's usual tidiness. His throat tightened. She must have been too upset to clean up.

Ajith's trembling fingers reached for the chapati she had left behind. He brought it to his lips, tasting the ghost of her touch in the food she had prepared. The familiar warmth of her cooking spread through him, taking him back to happier days.

"Remember when you taught me to make these?" he whispered to the empty kitchen. That first attempt had been disastrous—flour everywhere, dough stuck to his fingers. But Nilu had laughed, taking his hands in hers, showing him how to roll the perfect circle.

He sank into her chair, savoring every bite she had left behind. For a moment, he could almost feel her presence next to him, hear her gentle teasing about his clumsy cooking attempts. The sting of tears held back blurred his vision as he swallowed the last bite.

That night, Ajith curled up on the couch, his stomach full of more than just food. The taste of Nilu's cooking lingered on his tongue, a bittersweet reminder of the love he still carried, even as he pushed her away.

*****

One sorrowful day, Ajith decided to take a half-day sick leave and returned home early.

He opted for an Uber, fearing roadside safety checks and preferring not to drive in his state.

Ajith stumbled out of the Uber, his practiced drunken swagger hiding the real weakness in his legs. A dark luxury sedan, unknown to him, gleamed on the concrete leading to their garage.

His footsteps faltered. Something pulled him toward the side of the house instead of the front door. Through the living room window, he caught sight of Nilu as she spoke with a well-dressed man - Rudhir.

"I've always dreamed of seeing the world." Nilu's voice carried through the partially open window. "Being free, happy... everything I thought marriage would bring."

Ajith pressed against the wall, his heart thundering in his chest.

"But Ajith..." Nilu's voice cracked. "He's become someone else entirely."

Rudhir's hand trembled as he withdrew it from Nilu's. His eyes grew distant, lost in memories.

"There's something I need to tell you, Nilu. About college, about Niharika."

Nilu shifted on the couch, her expression softening.

"She was everything to me." Rudhir's voice cracked. "I took her everywhere on my bike - movies, beaches, those little cafes she loved. We'd ride for hours, just feeling the wind." He traced circles on the coffee table. "That final day... I was going too fast. The truck came out of nowhere."

His shoulders slumped. "Every morning, I wake up reaching for her. Expecting to feel her warmth, hear her laugh." Tears welled in his eyes. "The emptiness... it never goes away."

Rudhir's fingers curled into fists, his knuckles whitening. "After the accident, I couldn't step into our favorite restaurant. Her empty chair..." He swallowed hard. "The waiter kept asking where she was."

"Days blurred together. Food turned to ash in my mouth." His voice dropped to a whisper. "My sister found me passed out in our apartment. Three days without eating. Niharika's photo clutched to my chest."

"Rudhir..." Nilu reached for his hand.

"I need to apologize." He met her gaze. "Back in college, I helped Niharika keep our relationship secret. She wasn't ready to go public, and I... I let you believe I was available."

"Oh, Rudhir." Nilu squeezed his hand. "Some girls prefer privacy. Niharika was always reserved about personal matters."

"You're not angry?"

"How could I be? After what you lost?" Nilu's eyes glistened. "Life rarely follows the path we expect. I learned that lesson, too."

"I still dream of holding her, kissing her." Rudhir wiped his eyes. "Sometimes the memory of her is so vivid, I forget she's gone."

"That kind of love never truly leaves us," Nilu whispered.

Rudhir reached across the coffee table, his hand covering hers. "I understand completely. Missing your birthday? That's not love."

"It was the final straw." Tears streaked down Nilu's cheeks. "The only reason I stay is Anvi. She deserves better than a broken home."

Rudhir poured deep red wine into crystal glasses. "Here. You need this."

"He used to care about everything - my career, my drinking habits. Now look at him." Nilu accepted the glass with trembling fingers. "Marrying him was a mistake."

"You deserve so much more," Rudhir murmured, as he moved closer.

Ajith's fingers dug into the brick exterior, his knuckles white. Each word pierced deeper than any cancer diagnosis. The medicine bottle in his pocket felt like lead, weighing him down as his carefully constructed world crumbled around him.

Ajith stumbled away from the window, his legs barely supporting him. Each step felt like walking through quicksand as he retreated from his own home. The truth of what he'd witnessed crashed over him in waves - Nilu's tears, Rudhir's gentle touches, their shared intimacy.

His feet carried him to a small park nearby. He collapsed onto a weathered bench, head in his hands. The afternoon sun cast long shadows across the empty playground.

"At least she'll have someone," he whispered to himself, voice raw. "When I'm gone, Rudhir will take care of her."

But Anvi's face flashed in his mind - her wide, innocent eyes, tentative smiles, the way she still reached for him despite his manufactured cruelty. His chest constricted.

"Who will protect you, little one?"

He pulled the whiskey bottle from his coat, studying its amber depths. Not for drinking today - no, this was just for show. Just another prop in his elaborate deception.

The sun sank lower, painting the sky in shades of orange and purple. Ajith watched families pass by - fathers swinging their children, mothers calling them home for dinner. Each happy scene twisted the knife deeper.

With mechanical movements, he uncapped the bottle. The sharp scent of alcohol filled his nostrils as he poured it over his clothes, letting it soak into the fabric. He swished some in his mouth, careful not to swallow, then spat it into the grass.

"Perfect," he muttered, adjusting his disheveled appearance. "The town drunk returns home."

As he stood to leave, his hand brushed against the medicine bottle in his pocket. The real poison that was killing him was hidden behind a facade of self-destruction. He squared his shoulders and started the long walk home, each step heavy with the weight of his choices.

Ajith slumped in the chair across from Pranav's desk the following day, his shoulders heavy with the weight of yesterday's revelations.

"I saw them together." Ajith's voice cracked. "Nilu and Rudhir. In our home."

Pranav leaned forward, concern visible on his face. "Your latest test results came back. There's something we need to discuss."

"What's the point?" Ajith stared at his trembling hands. "I've lost her already."

"Listen to me." Pranav's tone sharpened. "If you quit drinking, start taking your medication properly, and focus on your health - you could have many years ahead of you."

Ajith let out a bitter laugh. "Years of what? Being the awkward bookworm who can't keep up with his wife?"

"What do you mean?"

"I was never good enough." Ajith's fingers clenched in his lap. "The quiet med student who could barely look people in the eye. I worked double shifts and bought her designer clothes, fancy jewelry—anything to match her lifestyle. But I can't be the charming husband she wants."

"So you chose to become..." Pranav gestured at Ajith's disheveled state.

"It was easier to get drunk than admit I couldn't handle social gatherings. Easier to seem careless than show how much everything mattered." Ajith's voice dropped to a whisper. "Now she thinks I don't care at all."

Pranav paced his office, running his fingers through his disheveled hair. "Remember when you first met Nilu? In college?"

"That was different. I was different." Ajith stared at his trembling hands.

"No, you were yourself. A brilliant mind who could recite entire medical texts from memory. Who spent hours explaining complex concepts to struggling classmates." Pranav stopped pacing. "When was the last time you helped Anvi with her homework?"

Ajith's face crumpled. "I... I can't remember."

"The Ajith I knew would've turned those study sessions into adventures. Making up stories about cell structures, drawing silly diagrams." Pranav leaned against his desk. "Instead, you're stumbling home drunk, too dizzy to even read her a bedtime story."

"I see how Nilu looks at her actor friends. Their confidence, their charm-"

"And what good has mimicking them done? You're losing yourself, Ajith. Your real strength was never in being the life of the party." Pranav's voice softened. "It was in listening. Really listening. Remember how you'd spend hours letting Nilu talk about her dreams? How would you remember every detail she shared?"

Ajith's shoulders slumped. "She used to say I was the only one who truly heard her."

"Because that's who you are. An observer. A caretaker. Not this... hollow shell you're trying to be." Pranav gripped his friend's shoulder. "When was the last time you had a real conversation with Nilu? Or helped Anvi understand a difficult math problem?"

"I thought they needed someone more... exciting."

Pranav pulled his chair closer, his eyes intense. "Listen to me. You're not losing her interest - you're losing interest in yourself. The Ajith I knew commanded attention without saying a word. People gravitated to you because you were the smartest person in any room."

Ajith's hands clenched. "That was years ago-"

"If you can memorize entire medical journals, why can't you remember everything about your family? The way Nilu takes her coffee, Anvi's favorite bedtime stories?" Pranav leaned forward. "You recite complex procedures without blinking, but you've forgotten the simple things that matter most."

"You love Nilu more than your own life - enough to push her away rather than burden her with your illness. But when's the last time you showed her that love?" Pranav's voice softened. "No one can defeat you when it comes to love, Ajith. No one knows her like you do."

Ajith stared at his trembling hands. "I've made such a mess of everything."

"The Ajith I know wouldn't accept failure, especially not in this test of life." Pranav gripped his friend's shoulder. "You've never backed down from a challenge before. Why start now?"

"But what if-"

"No what-ifs. You're still that brilliant mind who won her heart once before. Stop drowning yourself in excuses." Pranav's eyes blazed with conviction. "Show her the man who noticed every detail, listened to every dream, loved her enough to become her safe harbor."

Ajith's eyes narrowed as clarity cut through the fog of self-pity. His medical mind clicked into gear, analyzing patterns he'd overlooked in his spiral of despair.

"Rudhir..." He straightened in his chair. " With perfect timing, showing up right when my marriage seems weakest."

"What are you thinking?" Pranav leaned forward.

"He could have helped - used his influence to get me into rehab, arrange counseling." Ajith's voice hardened. "Instead, he's there with wine and sympathy, driving the wedge deeper."

His fingers drummed against the armrest as connections sparked. "I was ready to let go, thinking she'd be happier with him after I..." He shook his head. "But why rush toward death when there might be a chance?"

A familiar light kindled in his eyes - the same intensity that earned him top medical school marks. "Let them think I'm drowning in alcohol. Let them see a man losing everything." His lips curved in a cold smile. "While my mind stays sharp as ever."

Ajith stormed out of the house the following morning, clutching his travel bag for his trip to Singapore. Nilu's bitter words echoed through his mind.

"Running away again? Perfect! Go enjoy yourself while we sit here alone!"

The crash of shattering ceramic punctuated her words as a vase hit the wall. Anvi's bedroom door clicked shut upstairs, a quiet sound that cut deeper than Nilu's rage.

"I need this trip," Ajith growled, masking his pain behind anger. "Dr. Pranav arranged everything-"

"Oh, of course he did! Your drinking buddy enabling another escape!"

If only she knew. Pranav had found a discrete oncology ward in Singapore, far from prying eyes and gossip. The 'vacation' would be anything but enjoyable - rounds of chemotherapy, a delicate surgery, endless needles, and nausea.

A few months later, Ajith stood before his bathroom mirror, adjusting the synthetic hair of his wig. His beard covered the gauntness in his cheeks, disguising how the treatment had hollowed him. His fingers traced the surgical scar hidden beneath his collar.

Nilu's cold shoulder at his return hurt worse than any medical procedure. She barely glanced his way, speaking only when necessary about household matters or Anvi's schedule.

"You look different," she'd said flatly upon his return.

Ajith had shrugged, mumbling something about trying a new style. The truth burned in his throat, held back by pride and fear. How could he admit his weakness now? After everything, would she even care?

He took his pills discreetly, keeping up the drunk act. Better than admitting he was dying. Their growing distance was the cost of his silence.

# Chapter 7

# A Strategy for Survival

Ajith's fingers trembled as he dialed a number he hadn't called in years. The line rang three times before a familiar voice answered.

"Well, if it isn't the ghost of med school past." Thejus's laugh crackled through the speaker.

"I need your help." Ajith's voice broke. "It's about Nilu."

"The actress who stole our resident bookworm's heart? What's wrong?"

Ajith ducked into his car, away from prying eyes. "There's this Rudhir. He's... I need to know what he's planning with my family."

"You want me to hack his phone?" Thejus snorted. "Not possible unless I have physical access for hours. And his device unlocked."

"There has to be something-"

"Hold up, drama queen. I didn't say we couldn't get creative." Keys clacked in the background. "Ever heard of micro-surveillance? I'm talking tiny cameras and high-quality mics. Completely undetectable."

Ajith straightened. "You can get those?"

"Better. I can customize a new phone for your wife. Pre-loaded with everything we need." More typing. "Gift it to her, say it's an apology. Once she starts using it…"

"We'll know everything."

"Exactly. However, I have to ask — are you sure about this? Spying on your own wife?"

Ajith's grip tightened on his steering wheel. "I need to protect them, Thejus. Whatever it takes."

"The quiet ones are always the scariest." Thejus chuckled. "Fine. Give me two days to set everything up. And Ajith?"

"Yeah?"

"Try not to look so suspicious when you give her the phone. Remember - you're just a guilty husband trying to make amends."

"Thank you."

"Don't thank me yet."

Ajith pulled into a dimly lit parking lot where Thejus waited, leaning against his car.

"Here's the phone." Ajith handed over the latest model smartphone, which was still in its pristine box.

Thejus cracked his knuckles. "Give me a few hours. And these-" He passed over a small package. "Latest in surveillance tech. Smaller than sugar cubes, but they'll catch everything."

That evening, while Nilu worked late on set, Ajith and Thejus moved through the house like shadows. They planted cameras in light fixtures, tucked microphones behind picture frames, and wired everything to a secure server.

"Testing, testing." Thejus's whisper came through crystal clear on Ajith's laptop. "We're live."

The following day, Ajith skipped his usual routine of dousing himself in alcohol. He found Nilu in the kitchen, her movements stiff with lingering anger.

"I know I messed up on your birthday." He placed the wrapped phone box on the counter. "I can't take back what I did, but maybe this will show you I'm trying to change."

Nilu's fingers traced the ribbon. "A phone won't fix everything."

"I know. But it's a start."

In Anvi's room, he installed every game she had begged for. Her eyes lit up as she scrolled through the titles.

"Really? All of them?" She bounced on her toes.

"Consider it part of my apology tour." He ruffled her hair. "What do you say to a family day out?"

The resort sparkled under perfect sunshine. Anvi splashed in the pool while Nilu relaxed on a lounger, her new phone capturing every moment. For the first time in months, genuine smiles replaced forced politeness.

Ajith watched them both, his heart aching with love and determination. Behind his careful mask of redemption, wheels turned, gathering data with every passing second.

Pranav pulled a glossy membership card from his desk drawer at the hospital and slid it across to Ajith.

"Premium access. Four months paid in full at Elite Fitness down the street."

Ajith picked up the card and turned it over in his hands. "A gym membership?"

"Starting tomorrow, you're training with Marcus. He's an old friend who helped me get back in shape." Pranav leaned forward. "He knows how to be discreet about medical conditions."

"I can't just-"

"You can and you will. Proper exercise, strict diet, and your medication schedule - that's your new routine." Pranav's tone left no room for argument.

"Marcus will work around your limitations. Build you up gradually."

Ajith stared at the membership card, its silver surface catching the fluorescent light. "Thank you. For all of this."

"Don't thank me yet. Wait until after Marcus puts you through his infamous core workout."

Ajith stepped out of the office, stopping by the nurses' station. He put on his best troubled expression.

"Sarah, I need to adjust my evening schedule. There's this bar I've been..." He let his voice trail off, feigning shame.

"Ok, Dr. Ajith." "I'll mark you down for early release?"

Ajith nodded, planning his gym sessions to match his supposed drinking schedule.

Ajith stumbled through his front door, cologne, and whiskey fumes trailing in his wake. His muscles screamed from Marcus's brutal workout, but he channeled the exhaustion into his drunken act.

He knocked over an end table, crashing a vase to the floor. "Oops," he slurred, making no move to clean up the mess.

Anvi peeked out from her room and then quickly retreated at the sight of him—the soft click of her door locking twisted in his gut like a knife.

"What's that racket?" Nilu emerged from the kitchen, her face hardening when she saw him. "Again? It's not even dark out."

Ajith sprawled across the couch, deliberately rumpling the fresh cushion covers. "What's it to you? Not like you're ever home anyway."

"Such a perfect wife." He forced a cruel laugh. "Always so concerned about appearances."

"Stop it." Her voice cracked. "Just... stop."

"Why? Worried what your fancy actor friends might think?" He watched her flinch, hating himself.

Nilu's face drained of color. She turned away, shoulders rigid. "I can't do this anymore."

"Then don't." The words tasted like ash in his mouth. "Nobody's keeping you here."

She fled upstairs, muffled sobs trailing behind her. Ajith closed his eyes, his carefully constructed facade crumbling momentarily. The medicine bottle in his pocket felt heavier than ever, constantly reminding him why he had to push them away.

Better they hate him now than watch him waste away. Better to have a clean break than a slow decline. He staggered to his study, leaving destruction in his wake.

Later that evening, Ajith passed by Anvi's room ; the door cracked open just enough to hear her muffled sobs. He paused, his hand hovering over the doorknob.

"I hate everything," Anvi whispered to her stuffed rabbit. "Mom's never home, Dad's always..." Her voice broke. "I don't even have anyone to talk to anymore."

The rabbit's button eyes stared back at her as she hugged it tighter.

Ajith's chest tightened. Through the gap, he saw her curl into herself, shoulders shaking.

"I'm all alone." Her words pierced through his carefully constructed walls. "No one wants me around."

Tears spilled down Ajith's cheeks as he watched his daughter break down. His fingers trembled against the doorframe. All his plans, all his reasons for pushing them away, crumbled in the face of her pain.

What kind of protector was he, causing such hurt to the person he sought to shield?

Unable to bear another moment, Ajith stumbled down the stairs and out to his car. The key scraped against the ignition as his vision blurred with tears. He needed to drive, to escape the sound of her crying, to run from the devastating reality of what he'd done to his family.

The engine roared to life, and he pulled away from the house, leaving behind the broken pieces of his daughter's heart.

Ajith pulled over on a deserted stretch of road, his hands shaking as he dialed Thejus's number.

"I need another favor." Ajith's voice cracked. "A way to talk to Anvi without her knowing it's me."

"Like what, a secret identity?" Thejus chuckled. "You're embracing this whole spy thing, aren't you?"

"Please, Thejus. I can't..." Ajith swallowed hard. "I can't bear to see her so alone."

"Fine, fine. I'll set you up with an untraceable Discord account. Give me a few minutes."

Ajith drummed his fingers against the steering wheel, his mind racing. He needed to find a way to connect with Anvi and be there for her, even if she didn't know it was him.

His phone pinged with a new message from Thejus. "There. One secret identity, ready to go. I even gave it a cool name - Sentinel."

Ajith's lips twitched. "Her guardian, huh?"

"Figured you could use all the help you can get in the protector department."

"Thank you, Thejus. For everything."

"Just don't let it go to your head, hero."

Ajith ended the call and pulled out his laptop. He spent the next hour installing every game he'd ever seen Anvi play, his brow furrowed in concentration.

Over the next few days, he scoured the gaming forums, searching for any sign of Anvi's username. Late one night, he finally spotted her in a multiplayer lobby.

His heart raced as he sent her a friend request from his Sentinel account. The seconds stretched like hours until the notification popped up, and the request was accepted.

"Hey there," he typed, his fingers trembling. "I'm new to this game. Mind showing me the ropes?"

"Sure!" Anvi's response was immediate. "I'm always happy to help a fellow noob. :)"

Ajith leaned back in his chair, a genuine smile spreading across his face for the first time in months. He might not be able to be there for her in person, but through Sentinel's account, he could still be the friend and protector she needed.

And so, a new avatar was born - one dedicated to bringing joy back into Anvi's life, even if she never knew the man behind the screen.

Months blurred together as Ajith perfected his routine. Each day at 4 pm, he'd wave goodbye to the hospital staff, muttering about needing a drink. Instead, his car would glide into Elite Fitness's underground parking.

Marcus pushed him harder each session, building his strength despite his condition. After their brutal workouts, Ajith would collect his specially prepared meals from Nina, the dietitian who understood his unique needs.

"Your numbers are improving," Nina said, handing him the evening's container. "This is helping you."

In his car, parked quietly around the city, Ajith would open his laptop. The powerful battery pack hummed softly as he logged into the Sentinel account on Discord and in games, his heart lifting with each message from Anvi.

"Sentinel! You won't believe what happened in school today," her messages would start, sharing stories that made him smile despite everything.

They'd game together until eleven, her laughter through the headset more precious than any medicine. Sometimes they'd tackle homework between matches, and he'd guide her through complex math problems just like he used to.

Through his surveillance, he observed Nilu growing closer to Rudhir. Their lunch meetings got longer, and their phone calls became more frequent. The evidence of their developing relationship accumulated in his encrypted folders.

But what was another man's attention compared to the terminal diagnosis hanging over his head? Ajith checked his latest test results between Discord messages, tracking the slow progression of his condition. The numbers told a story of borrowed time, each month a gift he hadn't expected.

He'd catch a glimpse of Rudhir's polished smile in the surveillance footage, watch him shower Nilu with the attention she deserved. Part of him wanted to rage, fight, and claim back what was his. But the medical charts on his desk reminded him—what future could he offer her?

So he concentrated on being Sentinel and supporting Anvi in the only way he knew how. Let Rudhir play the charming politician. Ajith had more important battles to fight.

Pranav studied the latest test results, his eyes widening. "This is remarkable, Ajith. Your numbers have improved significantly."

Ajith leaned forward in his chair. "What does that mean?"

"It means whatever you're doing is working. The exercise, the diet - your body's responding." Pranav topped the chart. "You're getting stronger."

A spark of hope flickered in Ajith's chest. He pulled out his phone, fingers flying across the screen as he dialed Marcus.

"I need more." Ajith's voice carried a steel edge. "Boxing, martial arts - whatever you can teach me."

Marcus whistled. "That's intense. You sure?"

"Absolutely. Schedule it around my current training."

In the gym's mirrored walls, Ajith watched his form improve with each passing week. His jabs grew sharper, his footwork more precise. Some days, raw anger fueled his punches - thoughts of Rudhir's smug face driving his fists into the heavy bag.

In other sessions, gentler motivation encouraged him forward. He would picture Anvi's smile, her latest gaming victory lighting up their Discord chat. The daughter he couldn't hug in person strengthened him through their digital connection.

"Your stance is improving," Marcus noted, adjusting Ajith's elbow. "But remember - technique before power."

Ajith nodded, sweat dripping from his brow. His muscles burned, but he pushed through another set. Each punch represented a promise - to survive, protect, and fight back if necessary.

The training took up his free time. Between hospital shifts and his secret communications with Anvi, Ajith immersed himself in physical transformation. Each day, his body became leaner, stronger, and more capable.

"Your condition doesn't define you," Marcus said during a grueling session. "It's just another opponent to overcome."

Ajith smiled grimly, throwing a perfect combination at the bag.

*****

## The Shattering

Through the surveillance feeds, Ajith watched his family crumble. The screen flickered as Anvi crept toward Nilu's phone, desperate for an internet connection. Her fingers barely brushed the device when Nilu's hand struck her face.

The slap echoed through his headphones. Anvi stumbled backward, tears welling in her eyes.

"Don't touch my things!" Nilu's voice cracked with rage. "You think I don't know what you're doing?"

Ajith's hands clenched the steering wheel. His knuckles turned white as he watched Nilu grab Anvi's arm, yanking her away from the phone.

"Mom, please - I just need to finish my homework-"

Ajith slammed the car door, storming into the house. The sound of their argument grew louder with each step.

His key turned in the lock. The arguing stopped.

Nilu stood in the living room, phone clutched to her chest. Anvi huddled in the corner, a red mark blooming on her cheek.

"What did you do?" Ajith's voice came out as a whisper.

"She was trying to"

His palm connected with Nilu's face before he could stop himself. The phone clattered to the floor.

Anvi gasped. Nilu touched her cheek, eyes wide with shock.

"Don't. Ever. Touch. Her." Each word fell like ice between them.

Nilu snatched her phone from the floor. Her heels clicked against the hardwood as she fled to their bedroom. The door slammed shut.

Ajith collapsed onto the couch, the weight of what he'd done crushing his chest. Mufled sobs drifted from the bedroom.

The house settled into silence, broken only by the soft whirr of the air conditioning. Ajith stared at the ceiling, his hand still burning from the slap, as darkness crept across the living room.

The hospital corridors felt colder than usual as Ajith dragged his feet toward his office. His shoulders slumped under the weight of yesterday's events.

"Ajith!" Dr. Pranav burst through the door, waving a stack of papers. "Your results - they're incredible!"

Ajith blinked at the endoscopy reports thrust into his hands. The images showed clear, healthy tissue where the cancer had been.

"The treatment worked. You're cured!" Pranav's face split into a wide grin.

Ajith sank into his chair, the papers trembling in his grip. "I hit her, Pranav. I hit Nilu."

Pranav's smile faded. He pulled up a chair and sat across from Ajith. "What happened?"

The story spilled out - Anvi's tears, Nilu's rage, the phone, the slap. Pranav listened without interruption.

"So what?" Pranav leaned forward. "Talk to them tomorrow. Tell them everything - the cancer, the treatment, why you've been distant. And for god's sake, stop hiding in these baggy clothes. You're not sick anymore."

Ajith tugged at his oversized sweater. Beneath it, months of aggressive workouts had transformed his frame, a coping mechanism during treatment.

"You're right." Ajith straightened in his chair. "No more hiding."

That evening, he stood before his closet mirror in a fitted shirt. His reflection showed a different man - strong, healthy. He thought of Nilu's favorite **things,** flowers, and the little details he'd gathered over their years together.

But Rudhir's shadow loomed. After Niharika's death, he noticed how Rudhir looked at Nilu. The lingering glances, the casual touches.

"Not this time." Ajith grabbed his keys. He was determined to show Rudhir what real love looked like. He aimed to win back his family and rebuild what they had lost.

Tonight, he would hold her again. No more secrets, no more distance.

Ajith pulled into the driveway, his heart light with hope. The house loomed dark and silent. No lights in the windows. No movement inside.

"Nilu?" His voice echoed through empty rooms. "Anvi?"

His footsteps echoed loudly on the floors as he moved from room to room. Kitchen - empty. Living room - abandoned.

A faint mechanical hum drew him to the laundry room. The washing machine spun, its window streaked with red. His hands trembled as he yanked open the door.

Anvi's school dress tumbled out, soaked crimson.

"No, no, no." He fumbled for his phone, fingers slipping across the screen as he dialed Nilu's number, which was switched off.

He launched the tracking app - nothing. Her phone was dead or disabled.

Back in his study, he pulled up the security footage. The timestamp showed hours earlier. His breath caught as Rudhir appeared on the screen, entering through the door. Nilu rushed to embrace him.

Ajith's fingers dug into the desk edge as clothes fell away, and his wife melted into Rudhir's arms in their living room.

Movement at the top of the stairs caught his eye. Anvi stood frozen. She stepped backward. Her heel caught the edge of the step.

Ajith watched helplessly as his daughter pitched backward, tumbling down the stairs. Her phone shattered against the wall. Her body crumpled to the bottom, motionless.

Rudhir and Nilu broke apart. Panic flashed across their faces.

"We have to go," Rudhir threatened Nilu. "Now, before someone comes."

The footage ended. Ajith slumped in his chair, bile rising in his throat. His family lay shattered, and he hadn't been there to catch the pieces.

Ajith's legs gave out beneath him, sending him crashing to the floor of his study. His hands shook as he crawled to the cabinet where he kept his old monk collection. The bottles clinked together as he pulled them out one by one, stuffing them into a black duffel bag.

He yanked open his closet and grabbed a black garment—his motorcycle jacket. The fabric felt cold against his trembling fingers as he shoved it into the bag alongside the bottles.

The first bottle's cork popped with a hollow sound. He tilted it back, the liquid burning his throat. His mind raced with possible locations - Rudhir's house, old meeting spots, anywhere Nilu might have gone.

Another bottle was emptied. Then another. The room began to spin, but the pain remained sharp and clear.

Through the window, movement caught his eye. Nadia's familiar figure approached his front door, her face tight with concern.

"No... not now."

He stumbled toward the garage and snatched the last full bottle from the floor. The duffel bag dragged behind him, heavy with clothes and empty bottles.

His keys slipped through his fingers twice before he managed to unlock the car.

*****

Ajith slumped against Rudhir's front door, pounding weakly with his fist. The house remained dark and silent. He fumbled for his phone, his vision blurred by tears.

"C'mon, Nilu...pick up." Her number rang endlessly until the flat voice informed him it was no longer in service.

Ajith's shoulders shook with sobs. He clutched the phone to his chest, rocking back and forth on the porch step. Waves of anguish crashed over him, drowning out the world.

His family was gone. Torn apart by his secrets, his lies. If only he'd been brave enough to face the truth...

Now, his daughter's life hung in the balance, and his beloved wife had fled into the night with that serpent Rudhir. Ajith curled tighter, his cries echoing through the empty streets.

## The Gloom

Ajith leaned against the bar, his vision blurry from the drinks. The TV above flickered with breaking news, and his heart skipped a beat. His face looked back at him - a police sketch next to Nilu's glamorous headshot.

"Hey, ain't that-" A burly man pointed at him.

The room fell silent. Dozens of eyes turned toward him, recognition dawning on their faces. These were Nilu's fans - people who'd watched her shows, followed her career, and loved her from afar.

"You monster!" Someone hurled a glass. It shattered against the wall behind him.

Ajith's muscles tensed as the crowd closed in, faces twisted with rage. A fist flew at his face - he ducked, years of training taking over. His elbow connected with someone's jaw. Another attacker lunged, and Ajith swept his legs, sending him crashing into tables.

Bodies pressed in from all sides. He fought through the chaos, blocking punches and dodging bottles. His knuckles split against his teeth. Blood trickled down his temple.

He burst through the exit, stumbling into the night air. His car sat across the lot. Keys fumbled in shaking hands as shouts echoed behind him.

The engine roared to life. Tires squealed against the asphalt as he peeled away, leaving the angry mob behind.

Miles later, he pulled into an empty lot. The dashboard clock read midnight. His phone showed no missed calls or messages. Just the black void of Nilu's switched-off number.

One o'clock came. Then two. Three. Ajith sat in darkness, tears streaming down his face. His shoulders shook with silent sobs.

"I'm sorry," he whispered to the empty car. "I'm so sorry."

He'd failed them both - his wife, his daughter. All his strength meant nothing. They were gone, and he was powerless to bring them back.

The night stretched endless before him, each tick of the clock another reminder of his failure.

The phone's harsh ring jolted Ajith awake. His neck ached from sleeping in the car seat. The dashboard clock read 3:30 AM.

Nilu's number flashed on the screen. His heart stopped.

"Nilu?" His voice cracked.

"Ajith, I-" Her words came out between sobs.

A scufle. A sharp crack. Nilu screamed.

"Who told you to call him?" Rudhir's voice boomed through the speaker. Something clattered - the phone hitting the ground.

"Please, don't-" Nilu's plea cut off with another cry of pain.

"You woman!" Rudhir's words punctuated by the sound of impact.

Ajith's knuckles went white around the phone. His wife's sobs echoed through the line, growing fainter.

With trembling hands, he pulled out his laptop. The tracking app he'd installed on Nilu's phone loaded painfully slow. The signal bounced around before settling on a location.

The marker blinked at him from the screen - an abandoned construction project on the outskirts of town. The half-finished building stood like a concrete skeleton against the sky ;work halted months ago when political rivalries killed the funding.

Ajith zoomed in on the map, memorizing the route. His tears fell onto the keyboard as Nilu's cries echoed in his mind.

Ajith's hands trembled, Nilu's sobs still echoing through the phone. His breath caught in his throat, mind racing with images of what Rudhir might be doing to her. The tracking app's marker blinked mockingly on his screen.

Blood pounded in his ears. Years of medical training taught him to stay calm in emergencies, but - this was different. His finger hovered over the end call button.

A plan crystallized. Rudhir wanted to play? Fine. He'd give him a game he'd never forget.

Ajith ended the call and dialed Pranav's number. The phone rang three times before his friend answered.

"Listen," Ajith's voice cracked. "Someone just called me from Nilu's phone. He said he's Sentinel."

"What? "

"He's at the construction site near the old highway." Ajith cut him off, forcing panic into his voice. "Says he's trying to save them. Nilu and Anvi. I heard screaming."

Pranav's breath hitched. "I'm calling the police-"

"Don't call the police," Ajith's voice sharpened. "Sentinel said he'll kill them if anyone involves law enforcement."

"Are you insane? This is-"

"He wants an ambulance sent to the old construction site on MG Road. That's all." Ajith gripped the steering wheel tighter. "You have connections at the hospital. Make it happen."

"This feels wrong." Pranav's voice wavered. "What if-"

"It's my last chance, understand?" Ajith's knuckles went white. "My wife. My daughter. Please."

Silence crackled through the line. Ajith counted his breaths, willing his racing heart to slow.

"Fine." Pranav sighed. "I'll call it in as a potential accident. But Ajith -"

"Thank you." He hung up before Pranav could finish.

Ajith's hands moved with practiced efficiency in the dim car light. The fake beard that had become his shield peeled away, revealing the sharp angles of his jaw. Next came the wig - another piece of his carefully constructed facade dropping into the passenger seat.

He retrieved a sleek black motorcycle jacket from the trunk, still stiff with newness. The leather creaked as he slipped it on, covering his disheveled doctor's clothes. The weight felt right, like armor.

Under the streetlight, the full-face helmet shone brightly. It's time for Ajith to become Sentinel. I'm coming to save you, my love, just as your hero.

The kitchen knife slid perfectly into the hidden sheath he'd sewn into the jacket's lining. It's not his preferred weapon, but it would have to do.

Chapter 8

# The Last Stand

A roaring engine pierced the night as the black car sped through empty streets. Headlights cut through the darkness ahead. Behind the wheel, a masked figure dressed in black gripped the steering wheel.

The speedometer climbed higher and higher, the needle quivering as it approached the redline. The car seemed to fly, its tires barely touching the asphalt as it hurtled forward. The wind whistled past the windows, a high-pitched scream mingling with the engine`s growl.

Ajith's heart raced inside the car, adrenaline coursing through his veins. Hidden behind his mask, his eyes darted from the road to the rearview mirror, searching for any sign of pursuit. The city blurred past him, a kaleidoscope of neon lights and shadowy buildings.

He took a sharp turn, the tires screeching in protest as the car fishtailed before regaining traction. The man's breath came in short, sharp gasps, his chest heaving with exertion. Sweat beaded on his forehead, dampening the fabric of his mask.

The car hurtled onward, a black bullet racing through the night. He pushed the pedal to the floor, urging the car to go faster  until the world around him became a blur of motion and sound.

The black car screeched to a halt outside the construction site, its engine growling like a feral beast. The Ajith in Sentinel costume stepped out. He surveyed the building, his eyes narrowing behind the mask. He could sense the danger lurking within, the air thick with the stench of violence and decay.

He strode towards the entrance, his footsteps echoing on the cracked pavement. As he pushed the heavy metal door open, a cacophony of shouts and curses erupted.

Sentinel stepped inside, his hand reaching for the knife at his hip. The blade sang as it cleared the scabbard, its polished steel gleaming in the dim light. He moved forward, his body coiled like a spring, ready to strike immediately.

The first attack came from the shadows, a burly thug wielding a rusted pipe. Sentinel parried the blow with his knife, the clang of metal on metal ringing out like a gunshot. He spun, his blade flashing, and the thug fell to the ground, clutching at his slashed throat.

More criminals swarmed forward, their faces twisted with rage and fear. Sentinel met them head-on, his knife a blur of motion. He ducked and weaved, his body moving with a fluid grace that belied his deadly purpose. A stick whistled past his head, and he snatched it out of the air, wielding it like a staff. He cracked it across the face of a charging attacker, sending him sprawling.

The man was a force of nature; his every movement was precise and deadly. He snatched a pair of nunchaku from a fallen foe, whirling them around his body in a dizzying display of skill. Bones crunched, and bodies fell as he plowed through the ranks of criminals, his knife and improvised weapons dealing death with every blow.

The warehouse echoed with the sounds of battle, the screams of the wounded and the dying mingling with the clash of steel on steel. The man fought on, his breath coming in ragged gasps, his body slick with sweat and blood.

Sentinel's eyes scanned the construction site as the last criminal fell, searching for Anvi. His heart pounded in his chest, a sickening sense of dread rising in his throat. And then he saw her, lying motionless on the cold concrete floor.

Time seemed to slow as he raced to her side. He dropped to his knees beside her, his gloved hands trembling as he reached out to touch her pale face. A drip had been hastily inserted into her arm, a feeble attempt to keep her alive. But the blood pooled beneath her told a different story.

Sentinel's eyes stung with unshed tears as he gathered Anvi into his arms, cradling her against his chest. He could feel the faint flutter of her heartbeat, growing weaker with each passing second. A choked sob escaped his lips as he buried his face in her hair, breathing in her familiar scent.

From the corner of his eye, he caught sight of Nilu, tied to a chair, and her face ashen and her eyes red from crying. Her clothes were torn, her mouth gagged with a filthy cloth. The sight of her, so helpless and afraid, sent a wave of rage coursing through Sentinel's veins.

He gently laid Anvi back down, his hand lingering on her cheek for a moment longer. Then he rose to his feet, his eyes blazing with fury. He turned his head away, unable to bear the sight of their suffering any longer. A single tear rolled down his cheek, a silent testament to the pain that tore at his heart.

With a roar of anguish, Sentinel seized the nunchaku from the ground and hurled it at the last remaining enemy, his aim very accurate and deadly.

The weapon struck the man square in the face, sending him crumpling to the ground in a heap.

But even as the last criminals fell, Sentinel knew it was too late. The damage was already done, and the lives of those he cared about were at risk. He sank to his knees beside Anvi again, pulling her into his arms.

And then he saw him - Rudhir, standing behind Nilu with a gun pointed at her head.

Nilu's sobs echoed in the vast space, her body trembling with the weight of her mistakes. She had been foolish, blinded by her attraction to Rudhir, who had captured her heart back in college. She loved Ajith, but Rudhir was always special to her—a flame she couldn't extinguish.

But now, as she stared down the barrel of Rudhir's gun, Nilu understood how deep her mistake went. She had betrayed her husband, her best friend, for a man who turned out to be a demon in disguise. She wanted to speak, but her words were stuck in her throat, blocked by her tears.

Rudhir's eyes glinted with malice as he tightened his grip on the gun. "Don't move," he snarled at Sentinel, his voice dripping with venom. "Or I'll put a bullet in her head."

Rudhir's grip tightened on the gun as he stared at the masked figure before him. His pristine white suit contrasted sharply with the grimy warehouse surroundings. "Who are you? Why are you here?".

A low, haunting laugh echoed through the warehouse. Sentinel stood tall, his mask gleaming in the dim light. "There are few heroes born in this world." His voice carried across the space with unwavering conviction. "I am one of them, and my name is Sentinel. I'm here to save my Discord friend Anvi and her mother."

The statement`s absurdity made Rudhir throw his head back in laughter, though his gun never wavered from Nilu's temple. "Are you crazy?"

"I'm crazier than you think," Sentinel's voice dropped to a dangerous whisper, his stance shifting subtly as he assessed the situation. The weight of Anvi's unconscious body in his arms only strengthened his resolve. Blood from her wounds seeped into his clothes, each drop fueling his rage against the man who had orchestrated this nightmare.

Rudhir's perfect facade cracked momentarily, uncertainty flickering across his handsome features. The man before him radiated a deadly calm that made his skin crawl. This wasn't part of his carefully constructed plan - this wild card in a mask threatened to tear everything apart.

Sentinel's muscles tensed, his mind racing as he calculated his next move. He couldn't risk Nilu's life. The man was a monster, a twisted soul who had caused nothing but pain and suffering.

Nilu's sobs grew louder, her body trembling with guilt and despair. She had been so foolish, so selfish in her pursuit of love. And now, because of her actions, her daughter lay in Sentinel's arms, and her husband's heart was broken beyond repair.

He stretched languidly, his muscles rippling beneath his tailored suit. "Nilu... she's a fresh flavor, a tantalizing morsel I couldn't resist sinking my teeth into." His lips curled into a smirk. "And Ajith, poor sap, left in the dust as she moved on to bigger and better things."

Rudhir leaned forward, his gaze intense. "Here's the thing, my friend. In this world, it's every man for himself. We're all selfish creatures, driven by our desires and appetites." He spread his hands, a gesture of mock helplessness. "I'm just honest enough to admit it."

He stood, his movements fluid and graceful. He snapped his fingers. "I seized it, no hesitation. My happiness, my fulfillment - all that matters in the end."

The sentinel's laughter echoed through the construction site, a chilling sound that sent shivers down Nilu's spine. She stared in terror as he positioned a knife, ready to hurl it at Rudhir, his eyes glinting with a cold, predatory light.

"You know, I was so lost, so confused about what to do, until you opened my eyes to the truth," Sentinel said, his voice dripping with sarcasm. "This world is full of selfish, heartless people like you."

Rudhir threw his head back and laughed, a cruel, mocking sound that grated on Sentinel's nerves. "Suffer, you son of a bitch," he spat out, his eyes glinting with malice. "There's nothing you can do."

But Sentinel smiled a cold, mirthless grin that didn't reach his eyes. "Oh, but that's where you're wrong," he said softly, his voice barely above a whisper. "I may not be able to change the world, but I can certainly decrease the population by one."

He took a step closer, the knife steady in his hand. "I don't want anyone to know who Sentinel really is," he continued, his voice growing harder with each word. "And those who do find out... well, they won't be alive to tell the tale."

Rudhir's eyes widened in fear as he realized the gravity of the situation. He opened his mouth to speak, but Sentinel didn't give him the chance.

Sentinel whispered, "Bye-bye," before hurling the knife with deadly accuracy. The blade sliced through the air, finding its mark in Rudhir's neck with a sickening thud. Rudhir's eyes widened in shock as the knife cut into his throat, severing his spine. He crumpled to the ground, a gurgled gasp escaping his lips as darkness claimed him.

Sentinel turned to face her, his eyes still blazing with that cold, predatory light. "I'm sorry," he said, his voice barely above a whisper. "I never wanted it to come to this."

*****

## The Present Day.

Ajith shifted in his chair as Inspector Daniel's eyes narrowed, studying him with renewed interest.

"That bar fight," Daniel leaned forward. "Three men hospitalized. Impossible for someone in your condition."

Ajith's shoulders slumped. The facade he'd maintained for so long cracked. With trembling fingers, he reached up and peeled away the synthetic beard that had become part of his disguise.

"Stage two gastric cancer." His voice came out rough, raw with emotion. "I underwent aggressive treatment. Chemo, radiation, experimental therapies. The drinking act - it was easier than explaining the weight loss, the vomiting, weakness."

He pulled off the wig next, revealing a head of baldness underneath. "I'm in remission now. Have been for months."

"Why maintain the act?" Daniel's pen tapped against the notepad.

"How do you tell your wife and daughter you might die? That their provider, their protector..." His voice cracked. "I couldn't bear to see the pain in their eyes. The drinking act gave them something else to focus on, something to blame."

A commotion erupted outside the interrogation room. Running footsteps echoed down the hall. An officer burst through the door, face flushed.

"Sir! Breaking news - Rudhir's body was just found. He's dead."

Daniel jumped to his feet, chair scraping against the floor. Without a word, he rushed from the room, leaving Ajith alone with his thoughts and the echo of the slammed door.

# Chapter 9

# Expect the Unexpected

A sleek white car wove through the crowd gathered outside the police station. Camera flashes lit up the tinted windows as reporters pressed against the vehicle, desperate for a glimpse inside.

"Please, give us space." Nilu's voice carried through the partially lowered window. "I appreciate your concern, but my daughter and I need privacy right now."

The sea of fans parted reluctantly, their worried faces reflecting genuine care for their beloved actress.

Dr. Pranav pulled the car to a stop, his usual calm demeanor masking the moment's tension. Inspector Daniel pushed through the gathering of reporters and approached the driver's side window.

"Please, everyone - give them space." Inspector Daniel's authoritative voice cut through the clamor. "This is an ongoing investigation."

Nilu stepped out of the car, her eyes red-rimmed but determined. "I appreciate your support, but my daughter needs rest. Please understand."

The crowd's energy shifted. Longtime fans nodded in understanding, gently pulling others back. Within minutes, the mob dispersed, leaving only the quiet hum of distant traffic.

Inspector Daniel leaned forward across the table inside the station's private conference room. "When did you find them, Dr. Pranav?"

"We need some space." Pranav glanced at the closed door. "Let's discuss this properly."

The fluorescent lights cast harsh shadows as Pranav settled into his chair. His shoulders dropped with the weight of his confession.

"I'm sorry for hiding them from the public. It was Ajith's idea to keep everything secret. I know we might face arrest for concealing this, and I'm prepared to spend time in prison for what I did. Ajith is worth it."

Daniel turned to Pranav, his expression hardening. "You realize the severity of what you've done? Both you and Ajith will face serious consequences for interfering with an investigation."

Pranav's laugh caught Daniel off guard. "I'd take a bullet for Ajith any day, Inspector."

The words hit Daniel like a physical blow. His mind raced back to the interrogation room, where Ajith had meticulously detailed every aspect of his relationship with Nilu. The precise descriptions, the careful pacing - it all clicked into place.

"Ajith orchestrated this? He was buying time," Daniel muttered.

"Around midnight, Ajith called me in a panic. He said someone named Sentinel had contacted him with Nilu and Anvi's location." Pranav's fingers drummed against the table. "When I arrived at the warehouse, I found them all there. Nilu and Anvi were unconscious, and Rudhir..." He swallowed hard. "Rudhir was dead, along with several others."

"And you didn't report this immediately?"

"Ajith begged me to wait. Nilu needed medical attention, and he wanted her away from the crowds until she recovered. I couldn't refuse as a doctor - her condition was critical."

Daniel sat back, processing the revelation. The man who'd surrendered himself had orchestrated far more than anyone realized.

"Ajith isn't just some ordinary person who found his family and turned himself in,"

Pranav's voice cracked as he continued his account. "In the ambulance, Ajith... I'd never seen him break down like that. His hands shook while checking Nilu's vitals, tears streaming down his face as he worked."

The fluorescent lights buzzed overhead as Pranav pressed his palms against his eyes. "He kept muttering medical terms between sobs, checking and rechecking everything. 'Her pulse is stable,' he'd say, then break down again."

"'Their minds will shatter if we don't handle this right,' Ajith told me. His voice - god, his voice was raw. 'The media, the questions, the pressure. They need time to heal first.'"

Pranav's fingers traced invisible patterns on the table. "I started to object, but he grabbed my arm. 'Keep Nilu at your house,' he begged. 'Treat Anvi at our hospital. Give them the best care possible. I need Anvi to be completely healed before Nilu wakes up.'"

"The look in his eyes..." Pranav's voice wavered. "He wasn't just a doctor anymore. He was a husband and a father, watching his world collapse. 'This is my family,' he said. 'What I'll do has no limit under the sky.'"

Daniel leaned forward, his stern expression softening slightly.

"I know we broke protocol." Pranav wiped his eyes. "But I didn't see the man you're investigating in that ambulance. I saw someone whose heart was shattering into pieces, desperately trying to protect his family one last time. Maybe I'm weak, Inspector, but I couldn't deny him that."

Daniel's gaze shifted to the interrogation room window where Ajith sat, head bowed. The pieces clicked in his mind — Ajith's detailed account of meeting Nilu, their college days, and their marriage. He hadn't been stalling or avoiding questions about their disappearance. He'd been processing his grief, reliving memories while knowing their location.

"All that time in interrogation..." Daniel shook his head. "He wasn't worried about finding them. He was haunted by how he found them."

Pranav nodded. "The state they were in... it broke something in him."

Daniel stood, straightening his uniform. "This Sentinel character - we'll need answers about that. But right now..." He strode to the door. "Right now, that man needs his family."

The holding cell door creaked open. Ajith looked up, his eyes hollow.

"Come with me." Daniel's voice was gentle. "Someone is waiting to see you."

They walked through the station's back corridor. Ajith's steps grew heavier as they approached the exit. Through the window, Nilu stood, her shoulders slumped. Beside her, Anvi's small frame tensed at the sight of her father.

Ajith froze at the threshold. His hand trembled against the doorframe.

"Go." Daniel pressed the door open. "We'll sort out the legal matters later. Right now, they need you more than we do."

Anvi, her head bandaged, walked towards Ajith, tears streaming down her face.

Ajith's eyes filled with remorse as he looked at his daughter. "I'm sorry, Anvi. I'm a terrible father. I failed to love Nilu." He took a shaky breath, his voice heavy with guilt.

He ran a hand through his disheveled hair, his eyes distant. "When Nilu became a star, I felt I should have become as successful as her. I worked hard, never thinking I would lose her." Ajith's voice broke, tears welling up in his eyes. "I'm stupid. It's all my mistake."

Ajith's shoulders slumped, his words heavy on his heart. "Nilu was never mine; I can't even say sorry to you, Anvi. I want to die, but I wanted you to feel normal, even if I was an alcoholic."

As Ajith spoke, Nilu strolled towards them, her body shaking with sobs. Her legs gave out, and she collapsed, but Ajith ran to her, catching her in his arms. Nilu looked up at him, her eyes filled with tears, as she leaned on his support.

Nilu's tears fell like rain, each drop carrying years of misunderstanding. Her body trembled as she looked up at Ajith, her voice breaking with every word. "I... I know you don't want..." She paused, choking back a sob. "Want Anvi or me to know the truth."

Her fingers clutched at his shirt, tears running down her cheeks. "We... we were at the hospital." Another sob wracked her body. "Pranav told me everything."

Her eyes searched his face, filled with pain and regret. "Why did you... why did you act like this, Ajith?" The words came out in fragments between her gasps for air. "All this time..."

Nilu's grip on his shirt weakened, her voice growing fainter. "I forgot... I forgot how much you..." Her eyes began to flutter. "How much you loved me..."

Her body went limp in his arms, consciousness slipping away as the last tear rolled down her cheek.

"Why do you... think I want you to be..." She choked back a sob, her voice barely above a whisper. "...to be successful?"

Her body shook as she pressed more closer to him. "I don't deserve... forgiveness or any punishment in this world."

Fresh tears spilled from her eyes, leaving dark spots on Ajith's shirt. "People chase love, and I..." Her voice cracked. "I was attracted to Rudhir. But he was my dream guy who had... who had never been in my life."

Her hand lifted weakly to trace the contours of Ajith's face, remembering the shy college student she'd fallen for years ago. The tears wouldn't stop falling as memories flooded back.

"I was missing you... more than anyone." Her words came between shuddering breaths. "You were the one who... who cured my depression before."

Nilu's voice broke completely as realization washed over her. "I never saw it; I was... I was lost in my dream."

She pressed her forehead against his chest, her shoulders heaving with each sob. "I missed him because... because I never had him."

"But every day since you met me, you were in my life. Even when you became an alcoholic, I was missing a part of me. Rudhir was my crush, but you are not. You were half of myself. My heart shared half with you. My mind wouldn't work when you weren't with me. Everything I did was with you only. I am not an actress, Ajith. I am a part of you, and I never understood it. When I became famous, it wasn't because of me. You supported me. But when you wanted to prove that you could work hard to be like me, I was missing myself. I got Rudhir, but I lost you before you even knew."

Nilu's sobs intensified as she recalled, "Once when I called you, you were doing surgery day and night. When I wanted to discuss something, Rudhir texted me. We didn't want to talk, but..." She broke down, her body shaking with sobs. "I am nothing without you. I never knew you started drinking and working hard because of me. I will not act in films now, Ajith. I want to quit as a punishment. I never wanted to love you because I never thought of you once. I never needed to. Rudhir filled the gap that you made in my life."

Ajith held Nilu tightly, his tears falling as he listened to her heartfelt confession. The weight of their past mistakes and misunderstandings hung heavy in the air, but a glimmer of hope began to shine through. They had finally opened their hearts to each other, revealing the depths of their love and the pain they had endured.

Anvi watched her parents, her own heart aching for the suffering they had all experienced. She stepped closer, placing a gentle hand on their shoulders. "Mom, Dad," she whispered, her voice filled with love and understanding. "We can heal together. We can start again."

Ajith's eyes glistened with tears as he listened to Nilu's heartfelt confession. His voice trembled as he replied, "But you loved people like him, not people like me. I was never enough for you."

She looked up at him, her eyes filled with longing and regret. "I wanted my old friend who could cure my sadness. The one who was always there for me, even when I didn't realize it." Nilu's voice cracked with emotion as she continued, "I took you for granted, and I lost sight of what truly mattered. My attraction with Rudhir blinded me, but it was never real love."

Ajith's voice trembled with emotion as he held Nilu close, rain pouring around them. "I love you, Nilu. You are my only lover. I wasn't confident enough to say it before, but not anymore. I want you, even if..."

Before Nilu could hear the rest of Ajith's words, everything began to fade in front of her like a mist. The scent of alcohol felt like an intoxicating perfume. She couldn't hear his words, but her eyes were drawn to his lips and the beard that framed his face. Nilu's heart started racing, and all she could see was the sparkling intensity in Ajith's eyes.

His arms felt like a fortress, protecting her from everything. As Ajith's beard lightly brushed her face, Nilu felt butterflies fluttering in her stomach. She couldn't understand what was happening, but when Ajith's lips met hers, her heart threatened to burst out of her chest. All her weight melted into his arms, and she collapsed against him, surrendering to the overwhelming emotions.

The cold mist in the air mingled with the raindrops that fell on Nilu's face. She opened her eyes and could feel the water dripping from Ajith's beard and running down his Adam's apple. The rain enveloped them, and Nilu shivered, from the cold and the weight of her mistakes. But Ajith's warm embrace sheltered her, his body heat seeping into her chilled skin. Her heart pounded in sync with his, their rhythms intertwined in a symphony of love and redemption.

Nilu clung to Ajith tightly, her fingers digging into his back as she buried her face in his chest. The rain kept falling, washing away the pain and regrets of the past. In that moment, nothing else mattered — not the mistakes they made, not the heartache they endured. All that existed was the love that had always been there, hidden beneath the surface, waiting to be discovered.

Nilu's sobs echoed through the rain-soaked air as she clung to Ajith, her body trembling with her emotions. "I never knew what love was, Ajith," she cried, her voice cracking with each word. "I was so blind, so foolish."

Ajith's tears blended with the rain on his face as he held Nilu close, his heart swelling with a love he'd kept hidden for so long. "I love you, Nilu," he whispered, his voice trembling with the weight of his confession.

At the exact moment, Nilu's words tumbled out in a rush of emotion. "I love you too, Ajith," she sobbed, her fingers clutching at his shirt.

Through her tears, Nilu's eyes sparkled with a sudden realization. "I now know why you fell after you punctured my finger in the lab," she said, a hint of laughter mixing with her sobs. "I can understand why you became unconscious and fell. I'm so sorry, Ajith. I never knew what love was when you were pouring your heart out to me."

Ajith couldn't help but chuckle, his laughter mingling with Nilu's in a beautiful melody of love and redemption. "I was so nervous around you," he admitted, his eyes twinkling with mirth. "I couldn't handle the sight of your blood. It was like my heart stopped every time you were near."

Nilu's laughter grew louder as tears of joy and relief streamed down her face. "You were always there for me, Ajith," she said, her voice full of admiration. "Even when I was too blind to see it."

As they embraced each other, lost in the moment of their long-awaited confession, Anvi watched from afar, her eyes wide with wonder. She had never seen her parents like this—so open and vulnerable, their love shining through the rain like a beacon of hope.

Anvi's heart filled with emotion as she watched the most beautiful moment she had ever seen. Her parents, who had endured so much pain and heartache, were finally reconnecting. It was a love story that had taken years to unfold, a tale of missed chances and new beginnings.

But as Anvi watched, a sudden thought struck her, and she stepped forward, her voice small and uncertain. "Papa," she called out, her eyes filled with hope and fear. "Do you have anything left for me?"

Ajith and Nilu turned to their daughter, their eyes widening with surprise. They had been so lost in each other that they had almost forgotten about the precious girl who had brought them back together.

Ajith's face softened, and he held out his hand to Anvi, beckoning her to join them. "Of course, my little angel," he said, his voice thick with emotion. "I have half the love in the world for you."

Anvi's eyes widened as she looked at Ajith, her voice trembling with disbelief. "It's not enough, Papa," she said, her words cutting through the rain-soaked air.

Nilu and Ajith, still wrapped in each other's arms, couldn't help but laugh through their tears at Anvi's unexpected question. The absurdity of the moment brought a flicker of light to their heavy hearts.

Ajith turned to Anvi, his eyes full of determination. "We're going on a month-long trip, just the three of us," he announced, his voice steady and confident. "We'll leave behind our jobs, careers, and even your school."

Anvi couldn't help but laugh, her giggles blending with the rain still falling around them. She looked at her parents, her heart swelling with love and gratitude for the family she had been blessed with.

"Let's go on a trip in Pranav's car," Anvi suggested, her eyes sparkling excitedly.

Ajith chuckled and ruffled her hair affectionately. "What do you mean by car? I'm taking you to your favorite anime spot, Tokyo!"

Anvi's eyes widened, and she bounced on her toes. "Really? Tokyo? That's amazing!" She paused, considering his words. "But Papa, I want to go where Grandpa took you during childhood."

Ajith's expression softened, a wistful smile tugging at his lips. "Ah, you mean the Vaishno Devi temple pilgrimage. My father took me there when I was a child."

He gazed off into the distance, lost in memories. "That temple holds such precious memories for me. It was one of the best places to relax my mind and find peace. Whenever I think of my childhood, I remember those sacred hills and the serene atmosphere."

Nilu gently slid her hand into Ajith's, her eyes full of understanding. She knew how important this trip was to him.

Ajith's voice grew thick with emotion as he kept speaking. "My father once told me that I should visit the temple whenever I felt sad. He said that standing between the earth and sky, surrounded by the twinkling stars above and the sparkling lights below, I would feel like I was in the middle of the universe."

He swallowed hard, his eyes glistening with unshed tears. "He believed that even after his passing, he could hear me if I spoke to him there. It was a sacred place, a connection to him that transcended life and death."

Anvi listened, entranced by her father's words, her heart swelling with love and respect for her grandfather's memory.

Ajith turned to Nilu and Anvi, his gaze filled with determination. "I want to take you both there, to that special place. I want to show my father, wherever he is, the beautiful family I've been blessed with. I want him to see how far I've come, how much love and happiness I've found despite our struggles."

He pulled them both into a tight embrace, his voice thick with emotion. "That temple is where I'll find my childhood again, where I'll feel whole and at peace. And I want to share that experience with the two most precious people in my life."

Nilu and Anvi returned his embrace, their hearts filled with love and anticipation for the journey ahead, a pilgrimage not only to a sacred temple but to the depths of their family's bond and the healing power of love.

Inspector Daniel cleared his throat, breaking the tender moment between the family. His expression was a mix of sympathy and duty.

"I hate to interrupt, but Ajith, you must come with me." Daniel's voice was firm but gentle. "Playing with the police investigation, even with good intentions, has consequences. You'll need to spend a few days in custody."

Anvi's face fell, her dreams of their immediate departure crumbling. Nilu squeezed Ajith's hand.

"I understand," Ajith nodded, his shoulders slumping. "Just promise me it won't be long."

"A week at most," Daniel assured. "Then you can start your family trip. Dr. Pranav will also need to join you, given his involvement."

At the police station, Pranav met Ajith with an apologetic smile. "Worth it, my friend. Every bit of it was worth it to see your family whole again."

The week moved slowly. Nilu and Anvi visited every day, bringing homemade meals and sharing stories of their trip preparations. They plotted their route to Vaishno Devi, researched places to stay, and planned their itinerary in detail.

When release day finally arrived, Ajith and Pranav stepped out of the station into the bright morning sun. Nilu and Anvi waited by their packed car, faces glowing with excitement.

Pranav patted Ajith's shoulder. "Have a wonderful trip, old friend. You've earned this happiness."

Ajith embraced his friend. "Thank you for everything."

As Ajith settled into the driver's seat, Anvi bounced with anticipation in the back. Nilu reached over and squeezed his hand and her eyes full of love and promises.

The engine roared to life, and their journey began - not just to a sacred temple, but toward their future as a healed and united family.

After their spiritual journey at Vaishno Devi, Ajith revealed his surprise. Anvi's eyes lit up like fireworks when she spotted the tickets to Tokyo in his hand.

The neon lights of Akihabara reflected in Anvi's wide eyes as she dragged her parents from one anime store to another. Ajith couldn't stop grinning at her excitement, while Nilu snapped photos of every moment.

"Papa, look!" Anvi pressed her face against a shop window displaying limited edition figurines. "It's the exact one I wanted!"

They spent hours exploring the vibrant streets, sampling street food, and hunting for treasures in tiny shops tucked away in narrow alleys. Ajith surprised them both with his knowledge of anime, pointing out references Anvi had missed.

At the Pokemon Cafe, Anvi squealed with delight as character-themed drinks arrived at their table. Nilu laughed as Ajith attempted to pronounce the Japanese menu items, his accent making the waitress giggle.

"Remember when you couldn't even talk to me in college?" Nilu teased, feeding him a bite of Pikachu-shaped curry rice.

"Now I can't stop talking," Ajith replied, his eyes twinkling.

Their evenings were spent in Yoyogi Park, watching street performers and artists. Under the cherry blossoms, they shared cotton candy and stories, making up for lost time.

On their final night, they stood atop the Tokyo Skytree. The city sparkled below them like a sea of stars. Anvi nestled between her parents, their arms wrapped around each other.

"Thank you," she whispered, her voice full of contentment. "This is better than any anime."

Ajith kissed the top of her head while Nilu squeezed her hand. No words were needed as they gazed at the glittering cityscape. Their hearts beat as one, a family whole and complete at last.

The wail of an ambulance pierced through Tokyo's neon-lit streets, its sound echoing between buildings. Ajith's grip tightened on the observation deck's railing, the familiar siren yanking him back to that night.

Blood had soaked through his clothes as he stood over Rudhir's body. The construction site floor was slick with crimson and a thick metallic scent. Nilu's unconscious form lay crumpled nearby, her face tear-streaked. Anvi remained asleep in the car outside, mercifully unaware.

His hands shook as he fumbled with the mineral water bottle from his car. The cool liquid mixed with the warm blood, created pink rivulets running down his skin. He scrubbed frantically, checking his reflection in the rearview mirror for missed spots.

The garbage bag crinkled as he stuffed his blood-soaked black clothes inside. He'd planned ahead, keeping it ready in the backseat. His movements were mechanical- evidence of meticulous preparation. The weight of the wet fabric felt heavy in his hands, heavier still with the burden of what he'd done.

The ambulance's wail faded, but Ajith remained lost in the memory of that warehouse. His hands had moved with practiced efficiency as he stripped off the Sentinel gear, stuffing it into a hidden compartment. The vest, the mask - all evidence of his alter ego disappeared just as the ambulance's lights painted the warehouse walls in rotating red.

He'd barely finished when Pranav burst through the door, medical bag in hand. Their eyes met for a split second - no words needed. They both knew what had happened, what needed to be done.

"Help me with them," Ajith had said, his voice steady despite the tremor in his hands. Together, they'd carried Nilu's unconscious form to the ambulance. The sight of Rudhir's blood had been too much for her - she'd fainted away. Anvi, they'd moved more gently, still sleeping.

"Papa?" Anvi's voice pulled him back to the present, to the glittering Tokyo skyline. "What happened? You looked far away."

Ajith forced a smile, shaking off the dark memories. "Just thinking about an anime scene, this view reminded me of. Can't place which one, though."

Anvi's eyes lit up. "Oh! I know - it I know - it looks just like that scene from 'Your Name'! The way the city lights spread out below..."

"I wish I had watched it," Nilu laughed, squeezing Ajith's hand. "Maybe we can all watch it together when we return to the hotel?"

The warmth of her touch grounded him, pulling him fully back to this moment with his family, away from the warehouse's shadows.

The flight home from Tokyo felt different than their departure - lighter somehow, as if the weight of their past had been left behind among the cherry blossoms and neon lights.

Nilu's phone buzzed with scripts and casting calls before they even cleared customs. Her eyes sparkled as she scrolled through the messages. "They want me for the lead in that period drama we discussed."

"Take it," Ajith squeezed her hand. "I can manage our home life while you're on set." His smile was genuine, though his hands still trembled slightly when memories of the construction site surfaced.

Anvi bounced between them, clutching her new anime merchandise. "Can I visit the set? Please?"

"Of course, angel." Nilu rufled her hair. "You can help me practice my lines."

At home, they fell into a new rhythm. Mornings began with breakfast together, and Ajith cooked while Nilu ran lines and Anvi added dramatic sound effects. Evenings found them curled on the couch, critiquing Nilu's latest scenes or binge-watching anime.

Ajith supported Nilu's career, rearranging his hospital rounds to drive her to early morning shoots. The dark circles under his eyes faded as nightmares of Rudhir grew less frequent. Dr. Pranav noticed the change during their shared shifts, though he never mentioned that night.

Meanwhile, Inspector Daniel stared across town at the Sentinel file on his desk. The vigilante's identity remained a mystery that nagged at him during quiet moments.

But in the Ajith household, such concerns felt distant. Their home rang with laughter and love - the sound of a family healing, growing stronger together. Nilu's star rose higher with each role, while Ajith found joy in being her biggest supporter and Anvi's devoted father.

They had finally found their happiness, building something beautiful from the ashes of their past.

# Chapter 10

# Trouble Knocks

---

Ajith's phone buzzed in the quiet of his apartment. Thejus's name flashed across the screen.

Ajith picked up the call and inquired about his friend's well-being.

"Listen, I must tell you about when you were locked up." Thejus cleared his throat. "I tried accessing the Sentinel Discord account to find evidence to get you out. That's when I noticed Anvi's account was active."

Ajith's grip tightened on the phone. "What?"

"The messages weren't right - the pattern was off. My contact in cyber told me her phone was in police custody. When I heard you got arrested, I dug through our CCTV server. Found everything. The affair, what happened after..."

"You did what?" Ajith's voice dropped to a dangerous whisper.

"I sent the evidence through Discord to Anvi's account. The inspector saw it before I could delete it."

Blood rushed to Ajith's face. "You had no right. That wasn't part of my plan. You've destroyed Nilu's reputation!"

"About that..." Thejus's voice took on a calculating edge. "Keeping quiet about what I know won't come cheap. One core Indian Rupee should do it."

"You're blackmailing me?"

"Insurance. In case things go south. You'll need someone watching your back."

The phone creaked in Ajith's white-knuckled grip. "One core? Have you lost your mind?"

"I know too much, Ajith. About everything. Your choice."

Ajith stared at the wall, shock, and rage warring across his features at this betrayal from someone he'd trusted.

—✹✹—

# About the Author

I am Bijith, born and raised in Kerala, India. Since childhood, I've harboured a deep passion for filmmaking. My mother, who always had a keen eye for my talents, often reminded me of my natural gift for writing. Like many others, I pursued a conventional path, working at a multinational company in search of stability and security.

However, I felt a void somewhere along this journey - a disconnect from my true calling. It was then that I decided to dust off my old dreams and reconnect with my passion for storytelling. This book marks my first step into the world of writing, but it certainly won't be my last.

I prefer to let my work speak for itself, and if you're curious to know more about me, my upcoming books will reveal more of my story, one page at a time.